Change of Heart

Second Chances Book One

by Jennifer L. Allen

Melissa,
I hope you
enjoy!
♡ Jennifer L Allen

Change of Heart

Copyright © 2015 Jennifer L. Allen

All rights reserved.

Published: Jennifer L. Allen 2015

jenniferlallenauthor@gmail.com

Editor: Aimee Lukas
Cover Design: Pink Ink Designs

Dedication

This one's dedicated to my nieces and nephews.
Ben, Maddie, Ev, DJ, Gabby, Amelia and Thomas.
I love you all and don't you dare read another
page of this book until you're at least 18 years old!

Prologue

Casey

Fifteen Years Ago

"We're gonna be best friends."

I looked at the redheaded boy with the bright green eyes like he was crazy. He was a boy, and boys were mean, dirty and disgusting. I yanked my hand out of his.

"No way! Boys are gross!"

I ran away from him, full speed in the opposite direction. My house was right across the street from the boy's house. The only reason I'd gone over there in the first place was because there was a big truck in front of the house earlier that morning and big men carrying furniture. I wanted to see who was going to live in Sadie's old house. Sadie had been my best friend, but she moved. I missed her. Now that boy thought he was going to be my best friend. That wasn't gonna happen. I was never going to be best friends with a boy.

Just as I reached my side of the street, I tripped on an overgrown root and fell down.

"Are you okay?" the boy called out from behind me.

He'd been following me! I tried so hard not to cry. I was six years old, practically a big kid. Big kids didn't cry. And I really didn't want him to see me cry.

"I'm fine," I said as I tried to stand up but struggled. The boy held out his hand, and I took it even though I didn't want to.

"Your knee is bleeding," he pointed out once I was on my feet in front of him; he squatted down to get a better look at the damage.

I looked down, and sure enough, there was a nasty gash on my knee. And what made everything even worse was that my brand new white dress was dirty. There was blood on the hem and dirt on the skirt. It was ruined! I tried not to cry, I really did, but I couldn't help it. My knee hurt, and Momma would never let me get another pretty dress again.

"It's gonna be okay," he soothed, "are your mom and dad inside?"

I nodded, still looking down. I was embarrassed that I fell when I was running away from him. And I was even more embarrassed that a few tears escaped.

"Let me help you inside."

"I'm bleeding, not broken," I snapped.

"I know that. I just want to help you."

Now he had a sad look on his face. I'd hurt his feelings. Now I felt bad. I didn't like hurting anyone's feelings. Even gross, dirty boys. Momma said that's not nice.

"Fine," I said.

His face perked right up. His smile was big, and his teeth were very, very white. He had a nice smile. He stepped to my side with the bloody knee and wrapped his arm around me.

"Here, lean on me," he said. I did and together we made it into my house.

My mom was in the kitchen, and she dropped the dishtowel when she saw us hobbling through the door.

"Casey, what happened?" she rushed over and knelt in front of me.

"She fell," the boy answered for me. I scowled at him.

"Who's this?" my mom asked me.

~ 3 ~

"I'm Decker," he said, answering again before I could open my mouth.

I huffed, "I can talk, you know."

"But you don't know my name," he explained, his hands out to his sides like he was stating the most obvious thing in the world. It annoyed me that he was right.

"Well, it's so very nice to meet you, Decker," my mom said, ignoring me. "Thank you for helping Casey to the house," she added, beaming at him like he was the nicest boy she'd ever met. Maybe he was a little nice.

He shrugged his small shoulders, "That's what friends do. And Casey and I are gonna be best friends."

My mom smiled down at him and my grimace deepened. He was a little nice, but we would not be best friends. He was still a boy.

"Casey, what do you say to Decker?"

"Thank you for helping me," I muttered quietly. I knew better than to ever not do what my mom said, even if I wasn't happy about it.

"You're welcome, Casey." He smiled his big smile again. It made him look a little goofy when he showed all his teeth like that.

I continued to glower at him as my mom cleaned and patched up my knee. Decker stayed right next to me in the kitchen the whole time. After my mom was done, she sat us at the table with milk and cookies. I didn't know why she gave my milk and cookies to him, but she saw my frown and told me to share.

"Thanks for sharing your cookies, Casey," Decker said happily as he swung his feet back and forth under the chair. Every now and then one of his feet hit one of the legs of the table and it caused ripples in my milk. It bothered me.

"You're welcome," I grumbled back.

"You don't like me, do you?" he asked sadly, stopping the motions of his feet.

I didn't answer him.

"It's okay," he stood from the table, leaving his half-eaten cookie behind.

"Where are you going?" I asked, surprised that he was leaving without finishing his snack. Who doesn't finish their cookies and milk?

"Home," he answered simply.

"Why?"

"Because you don't like me." His face looked sad again. I'd hurt his feelings again. I didn't mean to be mean. And I actually liked his smile.

"You can stay and have milk and cookies."

"But you don't like me," he mumbled quietly.

"How about I try to like you," I offered, shrugging my right shoulder.

He smiled his big smile, and this time I smiled back.

"It's a deal," he said, quickly sitting back down as if I'd change my mind.

"But no more talking about us being best friends, okay?"

"Okay," he nodded, the small word muffled by the cookie in his mouth.

I didn't care what anyone said. I would never be best friends with a boy.

Chapter One

Casey

First Day of Senior Year

I've always hated the first day of school. At least this is the first day of senior year. Ten more months and I'll be out of here. I'm sitting at one of the wooden picnic tables outside of the high school with Jane, one of my friends from the advanced placement classes, if you could even call her a friend— she's more of an acquaintance. Between my studies and extracurricular activities, I don't have much time for friends. Jane and I are always in the same classes and often study together.

It's blisteringly hot in August in Charleston, but there's a light morning breeze that's oddly more refreshing than the forced air pumping through the school. Lord knows we'll get enough of that over the next eight hours.

"I can't believe we don't have calculus together," Jane whines for what has to be the tenth time since we'd received our schedules a few weeks ago.

"Be grateful you don't have Mr. Anderson," I tell her. "He spits when he talks. You got lucky with Mrs. Stevenson."

She seems to weigh the options, then nods. "You're absolutely right. Good luck with that."

"Thanks," I roll my eyes. I'll be sitting in the back of that class for sure.

I hear some giggling and whispering coming from behind us and resist the urge to turn around and look. People calling you a nerd or geek and otherwise poking fun at you goes with the territory when you are in AP classes. I'm used to it, though it never ceases to amaze me how easily people put others in certain boxes, especially in high school. Those people have a rude awakening in store for them when they hit the real world and are at the bottom of the food chain, they are in for a surprise—and not a good one.

"Excuse me?" a voice shrills from behind me. Jeez, can't she just talk about us behind our backs like all the rest and leave us out of it? I want to keep ignoring her, but then I feel a tap on my shoulder.

I turn around. It's one of the popular girls, a cheerleader if the high ponytail, spanky shorts and sports bra—at seven-thirty in the morning—are any indication. Carrie something or other. She'd transferred into our school late last year, so I'm not too familiar with her—not that her kind would ever be caught with my kind anyway. She's of average height, thin, tan, with blonde hair and blue eyes. She's gorgeous, just not in a memorable way.

"Yes?"

"Did I see you ride here with Decker Abrams today?"

I sigh. Of course it's about Decker. It's always about Decker with the popular, pretty girls. We've been best friends for nearly all of the twelve years we've known each other and it still seems to surprise people. I take a deep breath and remind myself that Carrie is new, so she probably doesn't get the dynamic. Heck, some days I don't get it.

"Yes." Decker has been driving me to school since we turned fifteen and our parents took us to the DMV to get our beginner's permits. His parents even got him an old truck to drive. It's big and red and old but he loves it, so I love it, too.

The brunette beside Carrie nudges her, and Carrie gives her a sharp glare. "Y'all aren't an item, are you?" she directs at me.

An item? Seriously? Who says that anymore?

"No, we're not." I quickly glance at Decker. He is across the yard talking with his baseball friends. He laughs and his whole face lights up. Then he meets my eyes and winks. I feel the heat rush up to my face, but it turns from a blush to anger as soon as Carrie opens her mouth.

"I didn't think so," she smirks, briefly looking between me and Decker, before turning to walk away with her friends.

"What's that supposed to mean?" I might not be as pretty as Carrie Whatsherface, but I don't appreciate snide remarks about my friendship with Decker.

"Casey," Jane urges me to shut up. She knows the routine: do not engage.

"No, I want to know what she meant by that," I snap.

I know what people think of me. I'm a plain Jane, no offense to Jane, of course. But outwardly, I'm nothing special. I know that. My appearance isn't terrible, but I'm ordinary. My blonde hair and brown eyes are plain, boring, normal. On the inside I am a total nerd...on the path to being the valedictorian of our class, even though graduation is ten long months away. There is nothing extraordinary about me. At least nothing the other kids in school had ever found interesting enough. Anyone other than Decker. And maybe Jane.

Regardless, it still ticks me off that someone would assume I'm not good enough for someone like Decker. Especially someone who knows nothing about me, and she probably doesn't know anything about Decker either.

Sure, he's the most popular guy in our class. He's athletic and smart—a double threat. Then there's his dark auburn hair styled into a short buzz cut and his startling green eyes you can get lost in. Quite contrary to my fairly bland appearance.

But none of that matters to us. Decker is my best friend, has been since we were six years old. We'd been inseparable through all our grade school years and every summer. We'd even celebrated every single birthday together once we'd realized we were born on the exact same day—Valentine's Day.

I bet these girls would never guess that I have a standing Valentine's date every year with Decker Abrams. What would they say to that?

"I didn't mean anything by it," Carrie passes on an artificial smile and continues on her path.

"Bitch," I mutter under my breath once Carrie is far enough out of earshot.

"What was that?" I jump as I feel his hands on my shoulders.

"Decker, you scared the hell outta me!" I turn and swat at him.

"Was she giving you a hard time?" he asks, nodding his head at where Carrie is standing with her friends. I look over just in time to see her give Decker a little wave and fight the urge to vomit.

"No, she was just asking about tutoring." I catch Jane shaking her head at my blatant lie, but she knows I'd never tell Decker what I go through on a somewhat daily basis. And other people are smart enough not to do it in front of him—or tell him and witness his wrath. The whole redhead temper thing apparently applies to guys, too.

He eyes me for a minute, clearly trying to determine if I am telling the truth. He finally sighs in resignation and breaks eye contact with me. "Okay. You still good for a ride home?"

"Yep, Jane's taking me home after debate."

He looks over to her and gives his signature smirk. "Thanks, Jane. I owe you one."

Jane flushes and looked down, quickly collecting her books. "I'm going to head to class," she quietly says to no one in particular as she hurries off.

I bump Decker with my shoulder. "You're terrible."

He laughs. "What?"

"You do that on purpose," I gesture towards Jane's retreating form.

"I can't help that the ladies love me." I shake my head. Decker is just as cocky and confident today as he'd been the day we first met.

I grab my bag off the wooden bench and Decker takes it from me, slinging it over his shoulder. We walk side-by-side to the front entrance of the school. "You better be careful, Abrams, or your head might not fit through the door."

"Ha-ha." As he's done since we started junior high, Decker walks me to my first period class. I know our routine will eventually change when he finds himself a girlfriend, and that's okay. For now I'll just enjoy every second I can get with my best friend.

"Thanks, Deck." I smile and turn to walk into class.

"Case, wait."

I look back at him, "What's up?"

"You'd tell me if anyone was giving you a hard time, right?"

Ugh. Why does he have to be so stubborn?

"Of course," I lie. "Look, I actually want to get a seat in the back in this class and they're going to fill up fast. Anderson's a spitter."

He nods, accepting what I've told him, but I can tell he doesn't completely believe me. "I'll see you later, Case."

"Bye, Deck."

I settle into the last remaining seat in the back corner of Mr. Anderson's classroom, surrounded by a handful of some of the smarter, popular kids. They all pause in their conversations as I walk past, then proceed to whisper to one another. I hear mine and Decker's names more than once and sink deeper into my chair.

I can never tell Decker what I go through on a regular basis—that people tease me and talk about me behind my back. Especially since half the reason they do it is because of my friendship with him. Not only will he get angry and call them all out, but he'll also never forgive himself for being the cause of it.

What Decker doesn't know, won't hurt him.

Chapter Two

Casey

Graduation

My nerves are causing my entire body to vibrate with tension and my stomach to roil. And it's not my imminent valedictorian speech that's causing it. I still haven't told Decker about my plans for next year, and I hate that I've kept something this big from him. It's the most life-altering thing we'll probably ever experience together, and I'm terrified. I'm terrified I'm going to lose my best friend. The physical distance while we're away at school will be hard enough, I just can't handle the emotional distance he might put between us once he finds out.

Is it wrong to want to live in the now with my best friend? My best friend with benefits?

Yeah...so that's a recent development. Recent as in it's only been seven months—nine months since our first kiss—seven months since...you know. They've been pretty amazing months, too. I'm so glad we'd picked each other for our firsts. I can't imagine any other guy I'd want to share those things with.

"Places, everyone!" Dr. Dean, our school principal, calls out.

I'm separated from my classmates—the irony of that is not lost on me—because I am sitting on the stage until I give my speech. I get in line with the faculty and guest speaker and patiently wait until we get the cue to file in. After my speech, I can sit with the rest of the class in first few rows of the auditorium.

Most high schools in the area have such large class sizes that they rent a local convention center for the graduation ceremony, but our school is smaller, more private, so our entire graduating class and our guests can fit comfortably in the school's auditorium. If the May weather in Charleston wasn't so unpredictable, we probably could have used our football stadium.

Finally given the cue, we file onto the stage and take our seats on the uncomfortable and ice cold metal folding chairs. I neatly cross my legs at the ankle and look out into the crowd. I know I'll never be able to spot my parents in the large hall, but I do know exactly where Decker should be sitting. I find him easily on the far left side of the first row—alphabetically he's second in our class, right after Julia Abernathy. I wish I could have seen him up close in his robe—I bet the dark green of our school colors really brings out the green in his eyes. He glances up at the stage and catches me looking at him. He breaks out his usual smirk and winks. I smile back and feel the heat hit my face...I'm sure I just turned eight shades of red right in front of my entire class and their families. I can't help it though, Decker just has that effect on me.

***

"There's my sweet girl!"

"Hey, Daddy!" I say as I finally spot my parents. I'm immediately pulled into my father's arms, then passed off to my mother.

"We're so proud of you," my mom tells me as she pulls back and cups my face in her hands. "Your speech was excellent."

"Thanks, Mom." I look around, outside of the school is a madhouse. "Where are the Abrams?"

"They're speaking to the Trents," my father says. "Should be right back."

I nod that I heard him. Mr. and Mrs. Trent are Sam Trent's parents. Sam and Decker are good friends and play baseball together.

Sam is the only friend of Decker's who is actually nice to me.

"Yes, Melinda and I need to take pictures of you and Decker together in your gowns since we didn't get any this morning."

I roll my eyes at my mom. She and Decker's mom have been taking our pictures together for every single event and milestone since we met all those years ago. I know one day I'm going to love and cherish those pictures—especially when we're far apart, but to do this right now, in front of my entire class, is kind of embarrassing.

"I'm gonna go look for Deck," I tell my parents and quickly step away. I had caught sight of him talking with a couple of the guys on his team, so I make my way in that direction. As I'm walking towards where I last saw Decker, it's not surprising that I hear Decker's name followed by an unattractive feminine cackle. Girls are always after him, talking about him, and drooling over him.

"It's going to happen tonight. Decker is finally going to see what he's been missing." The girl says, and I stop dead in my tracks.

"You sound so sure," another girl says.

"Oh, I'm positive. It'll make next year at USC that much more fun."

I look around for the culprit—the girl who is certain Decker is a sure thing tonight—and my eyes land on Carrie Miller and one of her clones.

"We got this close," she continues, holding her thumb and index finger close together, "at the last party." Carrie and her clone break out into a fit of giggles, and my stomach turns.

She's got to be lying. The last party Decker had gone to was last weekend. He spent the night with me after that party. He wouldn't have messed around with some girl—with Carrie—and then came over to my house. Would he?

I turn away from Carrie and head back to where I'd left my parents. I feel nauseated and confused and I'm not so sure I want to see Decker anymore. But I know the obligatory photos are unavoidable.

"Did you find him, sweetie?" my mom asks once I reach them.

I shake my head in response, not completely trusting my voice.

"You okay?" she asks. Damn mom radar.

"I'm fine. Just a long day. I'm kind of tired." I've always been honest with my parents about everything, so they have no reason to believe I'd be lying now.

"Well, you have time to rest up for the big party tonight," she says with a smile.

"I don't think I'm gonna go," I tell her, looking anywhere but at her face. She reads me way too well.

"Casey Evans. This is your last high school party. You never went to any while you were in school, heck, you never went out at all except with Decker. You're going to the party."

Why do I have to be the only teenager in the world whose parent encourages her to go to a party where there will undoubtedly be lots of underage drinking and other shenanigans? Especially one I really don't want to go to—not if Decker actually entertains his harem of women at them.

"There he is," my dad says, announcing Decker's approach. Decker is like the son my dad never had. He probably loves Decker as much as he loves me, if not more since they can do guy stuff together like fish, work on their trucks, belch, and beat on their chests. I do like to fish, but not to the degree that these two—three if you include Decker's dad—do, they're out on the boat nearly every weekend.

Decker throws his arm around my neck and pulls me in for a side hug. I wiggle in an attempt to get away, which is the norm, so he doesn't suspect anything is amiss. "Great speech, Case!"

"Thanks, Deck." I give him a small smile. I'm just shy enough that I get away with it since we're around so many people. If it was just us and my parents, Decker would have been all over me wondering what's wrong. He reads me too well sometimes, other times he's completely oblivious. "Can we get these pictures over with? I'm exhausted."

"Yeah, yeah," my mom says.

Decker and I pose just as his mom and dad walk back over. For the next twenty minutes, our moms take one picture after another. Here, there, and everywhere. Me and Decker. Me and my parents. Decker and his parents. Shots of us individually. As a group. By the time we're done, I'm certain more than one hundred pictures have been taken with various backdrops.

"You're coming to the party at Cade's tonight, right?" Decker asks after we've returned our caps and gowns and are heading to the parking lot.

"I don't know; I'm pretty tired."

"Come on, Case," he pleads, complete with his irresistible smirk and pout combo. "It's our graduation party!"

"Pretty sure it's Cade's graduation party," I say dryly.

He nudges me with his shoulder. "Last party of high school, come on. For me?"

I sigh. Surely Decker won't entertain Carrie while I'm there. Maybe I do need to go. Maybe I need to insert myself right between Decker and Carrie just to show her what's what. Not that Decker is mine to claim like that. We're just friends. Best friends. With benefits. The lines are always so blurry when it comes to Decker.

"Alright, I'll go."

"Whoop!" He fist pumps and picks me up, spinning me around in a circle and attracting a ton of attention before setting me back down. I smooth the front of my simple black dress and quickly look around at the gawkers. Across the parking lot, I see Carrie Miller, and I can feel her glare burning into my skin.

This is going to be a fun night, I think to myself as Decker boosts me into his truck, spending a little too much time with his hand on my ass. Not that I mind of course.

Chapter Three

Decker

By the time Casey and I arrive, the party is in full swing. The music is cranked and the bass is thumping, causing the frames on the walls to rattle. I make my way to the kitchen, looking for the keg. I'm dragging Casey behind me because I know if I let go she'll probably try to sneak out the back door. Not gonna happen. This is our last high school party, and she's going to have a good time if it kills me.

I fist bump Jimmy Lewis and give him ten bucks for two cups—one's for me and one's for Casey. She doesn't know it, but she's drinking tonight, too. I'd already promised both our parents that I'd call if we need a ride home.

Jimmy pours the brew, Budweiser by the looks of it, as I hold the cups.

"I'm not drinking that," Casey tells me, shaking her head with a disgusted look on her face.

"You are, too." She continues to shake her head and puts her hands behind her back when I go to hand her one of the cups. "Casey."

"Decker."

"Drink the beer."

"No."

"Casey."

"Decker."

"Last high school party, Case," I remind her with a sigh.

She rolls her eyes, obviously not falling for my attempt at peer pressure.

"If you don't drink it, then I'm going to have to drink both."

She growls at me—actually growls—and grabs the beer from my hand, muttering curses under her breath.

I laugh and touch my cup to hers. "Cheers."

She tips her chin in acknowledgement and takes a healthy swallow from the cup, then coughs and wipes her chin. "That's disgusting," she says, making a face.

I laugh and tell her to sip it slowly, then grab her hand and lead her out to the back deck where some of my teammates are. I feel Casey tense for a moment as we reach the crew, and I chalk it up to her being shy.

After quietly listening to me shoot the shit with the guys for a few minutes, Casey excuses herself to the restroom. I point her in the general direction of the bathroom, and she heads off, but not before I tell her she'd better not leave.

"Hot piece of ass, six o'clock," Beau, the team's catcher, says.

I quickly turn around, hoping he's not talking about Casey like that or I'd have to knock him to the ground. No, it's not Casey...it's worse. Carrie Miller. The girl is a barnacle. She tries to get me to sneak off to a bedroom with her at every party. I haven't entertained that thought once since she transferred here a year ago and I'm not about to start now. She's plastic, just like the rest of the popular girls. I'd figured that out when she fell right in with them her first day of class.

"Decker," her annoyingly nasal voice calls. I roll my eyes and turn back to the guys, but that doesn't deter her. "Decker, baby." She trips on her heel and bumps into my side, her red punch spilling all over the front of my white button-down shirt.

"Shit," I say.

"Oh no, I'm so sorry, Decker! Come on, let me clean that off for you." She grabs my arm with her talons and starts to tug me towards the house.

I yank my arm out of her grasp. "It's alright, I got it." I shake my head and start walking towards the back door.

"I'm so sorry," she sniffles.

Well, shit.

I can't stand it when chicks cry. Carrie might be a pain in the ass but it's obvious she's three sheets to the wind. Pity for her overcomes the disgust I feel and I awkwardly pat her on the back. "It's not a big deal," I tell her as I unbutton my shirt. "See? I have another one on under this." I take the shirt off and fold it over my arm.

She sniffles and looks up at me, her eyes scanning my plain white undershirt. "It'll stain," she says with a frown.

"Well I'm sure there's laundry detergent somewhere in the house. I'll just ask Cade where his laundry room is."

"I know where it is," she says, a little too perky all of a sudden. She grabs my shirt, hooks her arm around mine and proceeds to tug me into the house.

When we approach the stairs, I pull back. "Uh-uh. I don't think so."

She looks back at me all doe-eyed and innocent-like. It may have worked if it was anyone but Carrie. "The washer and dryer are upstairs."

I shake my head. It may be, but I'm not that stupid. I am not going upstairs with her. "It's not that big a deal. It's just a shirt. I'll wash it when I get home."

Standing on the top step, she's about eye-level with me. She yanks my arm, catching me off guard, and I stumble into her. She smiles and runs her hand, the one holding my shirt, down my cheek. I cringe and take a step back, but not before I hear a gasp to my left.

I close my eyes tightly, then open them and look over.

Shit.

"Casey," I say, turning towards her.

She shakes her head and pushes passed me, heading for the front door.

"Casey, wait!" I yank my shirt out of Carrie's grip and take off after Casey, ignoring the looks and whispers around me. They can say or think what they want, but I'm not about to let my best friend take off pissed at me. I follow her out the front door and down the steps. "Casey, stop!"

She finally pauses, startled by my tone, but she doesn't turn around.

I walk around to face her. "That wasn't what you thought it was."

"What did I think it was?" she asks flatly, crossing her arms over her chest and cocking her hip in a defensive stance.

"Don't play games, Casey. I wasn't doing anything with her. She spilled shit on my shirt and was supposedly taking me to the laundry room. Once she got to the stairs, I knew she was up to something and stopped."

Casey rolls her eyes. "Whatever, Decker. It's not like it even matters. I'm going home."

"It does matter," I insist.

"Why?"

"Because you're upset. It matters to me when you're upset."

"Why, all of a sudden, do my feelings matter, Decker?"

"What are you talking about? You're my best friend, your feelings have *always* mattered to me."

She visibly deflates, as if my answer has disappointed her. It shouldn't. She *is* my best friend. Has been since we were six years old.

"Listen, *friend*, if you're going to stay and drink, then I'll just take your truck home.

You can call me when you need a ride instead of your parents."

"Casey, what's going on?"

"Nothing, Decker," she says with a sigh, relaxing her posture. "It's been a long day and I'm tired. And you know how I feel about parties."

I nod, not entirely buying it. But I'll let it go for tonight. "You sure you're okay?"

She nods and gives me a poor attempt at a reassuring smile.

I pull her in for a hug and kiss the top of her head. "I'll call you later."

"Okay," she says quietly. I hand her my keys, she snatches them quickly and walks away. Without a goodbye. Casey never leaves without saying goodbye. I consider going after her, but stop myself. Something is definitely up with her and it's obvious she needs space to work it out. Casey isn't the type to hide. If she has a problem, she'll face it head on. So I know she needs time.

And I'll give her time. But not too much.

Chapter Four

Casey

End of Summer

I lie in my bed, staring at the text on my phone.

Deck: Still up?

I look over at the alarm clock on my nightstand. It's after midnight, and I have a long drive ahead of me tomorrow. At this hour, Decker only ever wants one thing. I know what I should do, but what am I going to do?

What's one more night, right? Does that make me a bad person?

Things with Decker have been strained, to say the least, since Cade's graduation party.

It's like he knows something is wrong but is too afraid to stir things up by asking me about it. I usually don't hide things from him. I've always been an open book.

But this...this I can't be an open book about.

Me: Yes.

Deck: Is it open?

He's referring to my bedroom window. His point of entry.

Me: Yes.

Deck: I'll be right there.

I roll to my back and stare up at the ceiling, the glow-in-the-dark stars shine back at me. Decker and I placed them there when we were twelve. It was only six years ago, but it seems like a lifetime ago. Things are so different now.

I hadn't been sleeping with him back then.

And I hadn't been in love with him, either.

Yep, that's right. I'm in love with my best friend. At Cade's graduation party, when I saw him with Carrie, it's like my heart had stopped. I'd believed what he'd told me—that it was a ruse to get him upstairs and that he stopped when he'd figured out what she was up to. But it was in that moment that I'd realized my feelings for Decker were much stronger than they should have been. And then, when he and I had spoken outside before I'd left that night, I'd realized my feelings were stronger than his, too.

You're my best friend.

Those four words were like a punch in the chest. But what had I expected? For Decker to have the big ah-ha realization moment at the exact same time as me? Not likely. Hell, my moment of realization wasn't even all that awesome. Since we took our friendship to the next level, Decker has never expressed that he wants us to be anything more than what we are. In fact, he'd always seemed pretty content to just keep our whole "relationship" a secret. Maybe if he would have just come out with it, his friends would have laid off with the teasing and the name calling. Or maybe it would have been even worse.

Then, to make the situation even more complicated, what do I do? I go and fall in love with him. Smooth, Casey. Real smooth. I've always loved Decker, but it's different now. Too different.

I hear the tell-tale sound of the window being raised so I roll onto my side to watch him climb in. Decker has been climbing in and out of my bedroom window for more than ten years, but it's only happened at night, like this, the past few months.

Regardless of the obvious strain, our appetite for one another hasn't changed. All summer long we'd feasted off one another night after night. It's as if I've been trying to quench all my desires before our impending separation. The separation he's still unaware of.

My heart pinches inside my chest at the thought of this being our last night together. Maybe, just maybe, things can be different. There *is* still time.

I take in his slightly disheveled appearance and my stomach clenches. He's really filled out over the past year. Thick, corded muscles in his arms and shoulders—natural for a pitcher, tight abs, and muscular thighs. Now another part of me is clenching.

He struggles his way into the room, then stumbles over to my bed. His auburn hair is slightly longer than last summer's buzz cut, but still quite short, and spiked in a messy, yet organized, way. He gives me a half smirk, his eyes are hooded.

Great. He's drunk. Just how I'd wanted to remember tonight. I should've said no. I should've ignored the text. I should've locked the damn window.

But it's Decker. My kryptonite.

"Have you been drinking?" I foolishly ask him, already knowing the answer to my question.

He laughs as he drops on the edge of the bed and starts pulling off his shoes. "A little," he admits.

"I thought you were in training." The frustration is evident in my tone—not that he'd notice in his present state.

Decker got a baseball scholarship to go to the University of South Carolina. He is going to be a Gamecock, and everyone in our town is so proud of him. I'm proud of him. Even though the baseball season isn't until the second part of the year, they have the team train all-year-round to some degree. And when he'd accepted the scholarship, he also accepted a pretty extensive summer training schedule to prepare him for what he will have to deal with once he is on campus.

"It's one night, Case. Stop being so serious all the time. It's summer," he slurs. He finally wrangles off his pants and shirt and flops down on his back.

"It won't kill you to take things seriously every once in a while." *Maybe if you took things seriously once in a while, you'd realize that life was about to change,* I think to myself but don't dare speak. I don't want a confrontation with Decker. Yeah...I'm a chicken.

"And it won't kill you to give it a rest every once in a while," he counters. And he's right. It is our last night together, the least I can do is refrain from lecturing him. It is too late for it to do any good anyway. Isn't it?

I sigh in acceptance, and he takes it as an invitation, rolling towards me and cupping my face. I look into his deep green eyes, and for a moment, I swear he looks sad. But he can't possibly be. He doesn't know what's really been plaguing me these past couple months.

He closes his eyes and presses his lips against mine. I pull him closer and he moves himself above me. My mouth opens on a soft moan and he takes advantage, pushing his way inside. Our tongues clash and our bodies grind against each other as we rid one another of our clothes, coming together completely one last time.

It's a night I will never forget. I'm so grateful that the bedroom light is out, and the moon is low so he can't see the tears I can't hold back in the dark.

"Decker?" I take some comfort in the heat radiating from his naked body pressed up against my back. It makes me feel bold. Bold enough to speak my heart? My mind?

"Hmm?"

"Things are going to change." I close my eyes tight, badly wanting to tell him everything. How much I love him...really, really love him. And that I'm going to Stanford. I want him to assure me that everything will be okay...that we'll be okay. That he loves me, too, and we'll make it work despite the distance. I need his strength.

"Nah." He yawns loudly, the liquor on his breath wafting over my shoulder as he exhales and pulls me tighter against him. "We might not see each other as much...but we'll always be best friends."

The small glimmer of hope I had burns out in the night.

"Best friends...right." A final tear falls from my eye, runs down my cheek and drops to the pillow with an audible plop.

"Forever..." he murmurs.

By morning, Decker is gone.

A few hours later, so am I.

Chapter Five

Decker

One Week Later

It's been one week since I'd last seen Casey. Her car hasn't been in the driveway, and she's not answering any of my calls or texts. Her bedroom window is even locked—it's never locked. I know I was drunk the last time we'd seen each other, but I don't think I'd said or done anything stupid. And she wouldn't be ignoring me if I did, she wouldn't shut me out. Casey would've given me hell for it. That's just the type of girl she is. She always calls me out on my shit.

I'd been too busy to catch up with her during the week because of training, but I'm not letting this go on any longer.

"Hey, Mrs. Evans," I say as I approach Casey's mom. She's unloading groceries from the trunk of her car. "Let me help you with those." I grab a few bags.

"Thanks, hon." She pushes the trunk lid down with her elbow and starts walking to the house. "How are you doing?"

"I'm doing well. Is Casey home? I haven't seen her car, and she's not answering my messages. I probably did something to make her mad again." I give her my best 'get out of trouble' smile, but it quickly turns into a frown when I see the expression on her face. She looks upset. "What is it? Is it Casey? Is something wrong?"

"I'm sorry, Decker. I thought Casey would have told you." She unlocks the front door and ushers me inside.

"Told me what?" Now I'm panicking. Where the hell is Casey? "Where is she?"

"She's gone, sweetie. She left a week ago. Last Saturday morning."

Last Saturday morning...the morning after the night I'd last seen her...she hadn't told me she was going anywhere. Come to think of it, she hadn't said much that night at all.

"Where did she go?"

"California," Mrs. Evans says, eying me as if I should already know the answer to my question. And dammit, I should know. She should have told me. What the hell is Casey doing in California? Vacation?

"Why?" I ask, feeling like an even bigger idiot.

Mrs. Evans looks at me curiously. "Didn't the two of you talk about your future plans at all, Decker?"

I think about it for a moment, did we? We'd talked about me going to South Carolina to play ball. But had we ever talked about what she'd wanted to do? I think back over our summer and even senior year and can't recall a moment when Casey had mentioned what she'd wanted to do after high school. I can't think of a moment when I'd asked her, either.

Things between us had been weird over the summer. We hadn't talked as much as we usually had. She had been keeping something from me. I'd thought she was just working it out in her head and would come to me when she was ready.

Shit.

Mrs. Evans saves me from further humiliation. "College, Decker. Stanford? She left for college."

"Right, of course," I nod. "I didn't realize she was already gone is all."

Bullshit. *I didn't realize she was already gone?* How about I hadn't even known she was leaving? Stanford? That's news to me!

~ 39 ~

Whatever rift was between us this summer, it sure as shit doesn't explain this.

Mrs. Evans isn't buying my crap, but she graciously doesn't say anything else about it, just nods in response. "I'll let her know you were asking for her. Her cell reception might not be all that great in the dorm." She'd probably added that last part in to make me feel better about her not answering my calls.

I nod. "That would be great. Thanks."

She smiles sadly. "You're welcome. Thanks for helping me bring this stuff inside."

"You're welcome. Well, I'd better get back home. Have to pack." I make my way to the front door with Mrs. Evans following behind me.

"Right, you leave next week?"

"Yes, ma'am, next Monday."

"If I don't see you before you go, good luck, Decker. You'll do great at USC." She smiles.

"Thanks, Mrs. Evans." I close the door behind me and walk across the street, back to my house, my mind racing at one hundred miles per hour.

It should be Casey sending me off and wishing me good luck, not her mom. I'd thought it would have been. It's always been me and Case. I can't believe she left for school and didn't even tell me. I rack my brain again, trying to remember a moment when she may have brought it up, but there's nothing. Not once had Casey mentioned Stanford or California. I would have remembered that. It's the other side of the damn country, for crying out loud. There's no way that would've escaped my notice.

I should have known. Hell, I probably should have asked her. Shit, she was the damn valedictorian of our class, of course she'd go to college. I've been so caught up in baseball between my last high school season, scholarship, and summer training. So selfish. Yes, I should have asked Casey what her plans were, but she could have told me, too. She should have told me.

We're best friends—or were. We'd spent almost every day or night together for the past twelve years for shit's sake. And she just leaves? I think back to that last night, again, trying to recall something, anything that might suggest to me that she was leaving.

Nothing. There's nothing. Not even boxes in her room. Everything had been in place. And there is only one reason why that would be. She hadn't wanted me to know.

What the fuck?

I knew whatever had been going through her mind back at Cade's party was a bigger deal than she was letting on. I fucking knew it. Now she's gone! Just like that. And I have no way of finding out why since she won't answer my calls.

I ball up my fists and try to reign in the desire to punch the live oak tree in my front yard. The tree Casey and I always used to climb. I used to shove the Spanish moss that draped all over it's branches down her shirt. Our stupid initials are somewhere on this tree.

How can she be with me like that and then just disappear? Twelve years!

I'd thought we were friends. Best friends. But I guess I'd been wrong.

I hadn't known Casey at all.

She hadn't wanted me to know her.

Chapter Six

Casey

Three Years Later

I'm on I-40, just outside of Little Rock when I get the call. I pull over to the side of the highway because I can't catch my breath. The words I'd hoped I would never have to hear play over and over in my mind as the sobs wrack my body.

"He's gone, sweetie. I'm so sorry."

He's supposed to be around forever. He's never supposed to leave me. This isn't fair. I should have had more time. I should've left days ago. I should've flown cross country to see him. I could have—no, would have—been there days ago. I could have seen him alive, one last time. But I'd always thought he was invincible. Nothing could bring him down.

How wrong I was.

I finally pull myself together enough to get back on the road and find myself a small motel to stop at for the night. I have about one full day left of driving, and that's pushing it, but there is no way I'm making any more progress tonight. Not if I want to make it back to Charleston alive.

The front desk clerk at the hotel checks me in very quickly, probably unsure of what to do with the borderline hysterical girl in front of her. I'm sure I look very attractive and sane with my red eyes and wet, puffy cheeks. And there's a good chance that something is running from my nose.

He's gone.

I sniffle as I thank the clerk and grab my key, then hightail it to my car to retrieve my overnight bag. Pausing at my car door, I glare at the offending backpack on the backseat—a reminder that not too long ago things were good. Things were normal. One of the most important people in my life hadn't been dead.

I had packed casual, assuming I'd be hanging out at the house and maybe the hospital if he hadn't been discharged by the time I'd completed the drive home. I don't have a dress in my bag. I don't have anything appropriate for a funeral. I hadn't planned on attending one. I'll have to go shopping when I get home. Right. Like I'm going to want to do that.

I unlock my car door the old-fashioned way—with a key—since my 90s era Civic doesn't have a fancy key fob. I grab the bag and slam the door, leaning against it for a moment to catch my breath. *How did everything get so messed up?* Shaking my head, I push off the car, hugging my backpack to my chest as I make my way to my motel room.

After three tries, the magnetic door latch finally gives and I stumble inside. I briefly look around the small, dark room. The bed looks clean enough, with its retro, multi-colored quilt. The shag carpet has definitely seen better days, but I don't plan on frolicking around barefoot, so I don't really care about that. The dresser is home to a small, tube-style TV and single-serve coffee pot. And there is a tiny bathroom with a walk-in shower. That'll do. It'll all do.

***

After taking a much-needed shower to rinse the road off of me, I flop down, face-first, onto the bed. I know I should find a restaurant nearby where I can get some take-out, but I don't have the energy. I lift up on my elbows and place my head in my hands.

I thought I had more time. Why didn't I leave after the first phone call? Why didn't I get in the stupid car and start driving right away? Because he wasn't going anywhere, that's why. He was always there. Always. He would never leave me. Why him?

Only he did. He did leave me.

The tears begin again, and soon I'm a hiccupping, sobbing mess on the horribly colored bedspread. I'm not sure how much time has gone by, but the room is dark and there's a faint buzzing sound coming from my cell phone on the dresser.

I stumble my way over. A text from my mom asking me to call her when I stop for the night. I can't call her now. If I speak to her I'll completely break. And I need to make it the rest of the way home before I do that. Before I dissolve into nothingness.

I send her a quick text saying I've stopped for the night and am already in bed. I do a screenshot of my location on the map app and add that I'll see her tomorrow. I strip the bedspread off the bed and lay above the crisp white sheets, curling my knees up to my chest.

When I finally close my eyes, all I see are the bright green eyes I've spent the past three years trying to forget.

***

After a terrible night of sleep, or lack thereof, I hit the road around four in the morning. My old school GPS indicates I have about thirteen hours to go, so I assume I'll be home by six if I keep my stops to a minimum.

The rest of Arkansas, Mississippi, Alabama, and Georgia fly by in a blur of trees and pavement, with only a handful of pit stops for gas and bathroom breaks. My car is littered with empty water and Gatorade bottles, as well as an assortment of chip and candy bags. I make a mental note to stop and clean it out before I get home. My mother will freak out at my junk food diet, and now is clearly not the time to concern her with my health.

As I drive down I-26, nearing home, I wonder just how different everything will be. Will his truck still be in the driveway? His boots on the front porch? Or will everything already be void of his memory? Kind of like how my heart feels right this moment. Empty.

I shake off the negative thoughts, I have thirty minutes left to drive. Thirty minutes until I can truly let loose the emotions I've bottled up inside since leaving the motel in Arkansas. Thirty minutes until I'm home, forced to face reality. To face him. To face the lack of him.

Once I'm in the service area, I turn on one of the local radio stations and advertisements for businesses that used to be familiar to me start playing through the speakers. I try to sing along to some of the rock songs that play in an attempt to distract myself, but as each mile marker goes by, I get more and more tense.

Pretty soon I'm pulling into the subdivision I grew up in. Everything is the same, yet so, so different. And there are some things that will simply never be the same. I turn onto my parents' street and try not to look at the house across the road, but I can't not see his big, red truck in the driveway. I'd always poked fun at him for that monstrosity. But I loved that damn truck. Almost as much as he had.

I pull in my parents' driveway, behind my dad's truck. Tears burn behind my eyelids as I put the car in park, and I can't stop them from spilling. I don't have to anymore because I'm finally here.

After three years, I'm home.

Chapter Seven

Decker

You've got to be fucking kidding me. What the hell is she doing here?

What are the chances that the one weekend I decide to come home and surprise my mom and dad is the same weekend Casey actually shows up? Three fucking years I've managed to avoid her, though from what my mom has said, she doesn't even come home. Her parents always go to California to see her. That's rich. Disappears without a damn trace and is too chicken shit to show her face back here.

Until now.

Three years and I still don't know what the fuck I did to make her leave so abruptly. Three years is a long damn time to be holding a grudge, but to me, it's valid. Twelve years we spent together, side-by-side, and bam! One day...she's just gone.

Well, I'll be damned if I let another day go by without telling her just how I feel about her sudden fucking departure from my life.

I storm out the front door and down the steps into the grass. She hasn't gotten out of her car yet, so I know I'll catch her before she disappears inside the house to hide. I look through the rear window of her car as I approach and it looks like she has her head down, probably trying to psych herself up. She always had to give herself little pep talks before big moments, and I'm sure being home after almost three years is a big damn moment.

Just as I approach the driver's side door, it pops open. I take a startled step back, just as she looks up at me.

What the hell?

"Casey? Case, what's wrong?" All traces of my anger are obliterated as I take in her wet, swollen face. She's been crying. And not just a few tears, but rivers of them. Her eyes are red and puffy and the top of her t-shirt has been soaked through. She looks fragile—broken.

Nowhere in front of me is the girl I used to know. This Casey is a stranger. If she hadn't shown up in her car, I wouldn't have known it was her. Not at first. She's pale, so pale. And thin. She was always thin, but this...this is something else. She looks gaunt. Unhealthy. Wrong.

A sob breaks free from her, and I fall to my knees, pulling her out of the car and onto my lap. My protective instincts have taken over and all I want to do is take care of her and make her feel better. I need to fix what's broken. My arms are wrapped around her, holding her tight to my chest as she cries. She's wailing now, like a wounded animal, and I have no idea what to do. She's gripping my arms, the only sign that I might be doing something right here.

"Casey? Baby? Talk to me, please? I don't know what to do here." I beg and plead for her to give me some kind of sign. Some inkling as to what is wrong. She doesn't respond, just continues to cry and shudder in my lap, her arms desperately gripping mine.

After a few minutes, she finally settles down a bit. Her breaths are coming in short pants, but the tears have subsided. She pulls away from me slightly and looks into my eyes, like she's realizing who I am for the first time. And she looks *pained* to see me. *She* looks pained to see *me*.

"I'm sorry, Decker," she mutters as she pulls herself completely out of my embrace and stands up. I let her go. I don't know what just happened, but I don't want to upset her further. I want her to feel comfortable with me...to talk to me.

But when she turns to go to the house without another word, that's when I've had enough.

"What the fuck, Casey?" I shout at her retreating back. Her slight jump is the only indication she's even heard me as she continues walking away, faster now.

Not this time.

I get to my feet and quickly run after her, grabbing her arm and spinning her around to face me. "You are *not* walking away from me. We need to talk."

She tries to tug her arm from my grasp, refusing to make eye contact or even acknowledge my presence or my words. "You're hurting me," she cries.

"Stop twisting and it wouldn't hurt," I bite out. She stops resisting and I let go of her arm. "You have to talk to me, Casey. You can't just show up out of the blue, crying your eyes out and not say anything. You can't keep blowing me off! I deserve better than that, damn it."

Her lower lip quivers and part of me, the part of me who was best friends with this girl for so long, feels awful for attacking her like this. But the other part of me, the part of me that she abandoned, doesn't care. He wants to know why she left, and why, all of a sudden, she's back.

"Not now. Please just let me go inside, Decker." She looks worn out, completely defeated.

"Fine," I say, clenching my jaw. "But we will talk before you skip town again."

She nods absently, almost robotically.

"What's happened to you?" I whisper. The Casey I knew was full of life. She'd been a little bit of a geek, but she was my geek. This Casey is lifeless. Emotionless, aside from that breakdown of course.

She meets my eyes so quickly I almost miss the movement entirely. Shaking her head she turns towards the house.

"Decker? Casey? Is that you?"

Casey and I both turn our heads, taking in my mom's quick approach from across the street. I hadn't even heard her car pull up. She completely bypasses me and pulls Casey into her arms. Casey immediately starts sobbing again.

What the fuck?

"Have I entered some kind of alternate universe here?" I ask no one in particular.

Here's my mom, who hasn't seen me in a good month, and she just runs right to the girl who devastated me when I was eighteen.

My mom was there. She saw what Casey's disappearing act did to me. Whether I admitted it at the time or not, she's my mom, she knew.

My mom pulls away from Casey and holds her at arm's length. "How was your drive? You must be exhausted."

"You knew she was coming?" I can't even believe this.

My mom shoots me a glare, but behind it is utter sadness. She's been crying, too. "You should try answering your phone."

"It died...I wanted to surprise you." I'd been on a road trip with the baseball team for the past seven days and I'd left my cell phone charger at the dorm. I ran into the dorm long enough to swap out my overnight bag, but I didn't have time to charge my phone and I don't have an in-car charger. My mom had my schedule. She knew how to get in touch with the team should an emergency come up, all the parents did.

"Will someone please tell me what the hell is going on?" I shout.

My mom glares at me again and turns Casey towards her house. "Come on, sweetie. Let's get you inside." She looks at me over her shoulder, "Wait for me at the house."

I watch my mom walk Casey into her house, wondering where her parents are. Did something happen to Mr. and Mrs. Evans?

That could explain why she's home and why she's so upset. Why my mom's upset. The thought causes a heavy weight to press against my chest. Mr. and Mrs. Evans are like second parents to me, have been since we moved to this street fifteen years ago. I hope nothing's happened to them.

God...I was such an asshole to Casey. I was such an asshole and obviously something must have happened to bring her back here and have her so upset. I just couldn't see past my own anger over her leaving to even begin to process that something might have truly been wrong.

Shit. What did I do?

***

An hour later my mom finally walks into the side door to the kitchen. I jump up from my seat at the kitchen table and approach her.

She looks at me and sighs, shaking her head. "Mr. Evans died yesterday."

Her voice breaks along with my heart. The air whooshes out of my lungs. Fuck. Fuck fuck fuck. I slowly back up and sit back down in the chair.

"What happened?" I whisper, my eyes wide and unfocused as I try to absorb what she's just told me.

"He had a heart attack, five days ago. They did an angioplasty and everything seemed to

~ 55 ~

be okay, fixed even. Then things went sour yesterday, he had another heart attack and didn't make it."

I run my hands through my hair and down my face. I'd just seen Mr. Evans two weeks ago when he and my dad drove up for a game. They were tailgating and having a great time. He'd looked fine. He didn't look sick.

Oh God. Casey! She didn't get to see him before he'd passed. She was probably on her way, thinking she was going to visit him at the hospital. No wonder she was inconsolable. I look back to my mom, and she knows what I'm thinking.

"She's resting. You can go see her tomorrow. Let her rest today. She needs to be with her mom right now."

I nod my assent, knowing that as soon as I can, I'll be climbing in Casey's bedroom window. Tonight.

Chapter Eight

Casey

Decker's mom stayed with me until my mom returned from the funeral home. I'd wanted to meet her there, but Mrs. Abrams insisted that I rest after the long drive and emotional couple of days. Once she'd gotten home, my mom and I huddled on the couch and cried for what felt like hours before retreating to bed.

And now here I lay. I can't sleep, and I feel like I can't possibly cry another tear. I feel numb. Like all the feelings and emotions I'd had in me have been cried out.

I hadn't been expecting to see Decker when I got to the house this evening. I'd assumed he would still be at school. The baseball season isn't over yet and the coaches were strict outside of the season, I could only imagine how brutal they were during the season. It was a surprise...for both of us.

The look on his face when he'd first seen me was pure anger. Not that I can blame him. Decker has every right to be angry with me. But when he'd seen my face...my tears...it was like a switch had been flipped. He'd automatically fallen into his former role as best friend and for that I am grateful. I know we'll have to duke it out eventually, but not today, thank God. I can't handle much more today.

He'd looked really good. Better than the last time I saw him. I let out a small laugh. The last time I'd seen him had been right here, in my room. He'd been drunk that night, but he was still Decker. Memories of our last night together roll through my mind, it's all so bittersweet.

Knowing what I know now, I don't regret leaving the way I had. Sure, I'd regretted it at first and planned to make it right at Thanksgiving—beg his forgiveness, but then things happened that had changed the way I looked at everything. Those things still have an effect on my day-to-day life. I've missed Decker every day and nothing will ever change that, but I can't regret the decisions I'd made that summer. Not with knowing what I know now.

I lay on my bed, staring at those damn glow-in-the-dark stars. Things really do have a way of coming full circle, don't they?

I hear a familiar sound. Still familiar even though it's been nearly three years.

"You left it open," he says.

"Old habits die hard, I guess," I say, still staring up at the stars on my ceiling. I vaguely recall having flipped the lock on the window when I had come into my room hours before. It had been automatic...a reflex.

Keep telling yourself that, Casey.

He takes off his shoes and slides onto the bed beside me, still fully clothed. That's new. I roll onto my side, my back facing him, and he pulls me back into his chest, wrapping his arm around my middle. I close my eyes at the instant comfort it brings and will the tears not to return.

"I'm so sorry about your dad, Case. I didn't know. Mom told me when she got home."

I'd figured he didn't known about my dad's passing. He never would have behaved the way that he did if he had known. Even if I did deserve it. Decker just isn't like that.

"I know; it's okay." I squeeze the hand he has wrapped around me.

"It's not okay. I was awful to you," he argues, pulling me even closer, as if he's afraid I will disappear again if he lets go.

"I deserved it," I say, feeling myself crack a little on the inside.

"You didn't, not today."

I sigh. Maybe not today, but one day.

"We will talk about what happened after graduation, Casey. Not tonight...not until you're ready. But it will happen before you leave again."

I nod, knowing it's unavoidable. He deserves something. Maybe not the whole truth, but some truth. We lay in silence for several minutes, listening to the sounds of crickets and frogs in the night. My mind's swirling with a million thoughts, most of them memories of my dad.

I sniffle, and he tightens his arm around me. "I just can't believe he's gone."

I hear him sniff and know that he's fighting some emotion as well. "I know. I can't either."

He whispers soothing little nothings into my ear as I cry for my dad. I cry for the memories I'll never forget and the ones I'll never get to make. The moments of my life he will no longer be there for. I cry for my mom because when all is said and done, she'll be alone.

"So...how do you like Stanford?" he asks me several minutes later, once I've calmed down. Surprisingly, his tone holds no bitterness.

I smile a little, this is something I can talk about. "I love it. It's everything I dreamed college would be."

"What are you studying?"

"Psychology. I hope to be a counselor someday."

"You always were so smart, Casey. You can be anything you want to be."

Despite the warmth his kind words send through my body, the smile leaves my face. "Right." If he picks up on the change in my demeanor, he doesn't say anything, and I kind of love him for that.

"You like California?"

"I do," I tell him, silently appreciating the segue. "I really like being in the Bay Area. San Francisco is lovely. The Golden Gate Bridge is more beautiful in person than in pictures. There are so many great restaurants and things to do."

He laughs quietly, "Sounds like you love it."

"I do. What about you? How's school? Baseball? I was surprised to see you home in the middle of the season."

He sighs and rolls onto his back. I immediately miss his warmth and a chill runs through me as I get the impression that what I am about to hear isn't going to be good.

"School is great. I really like USC. I've had a lot of fun, and it's nice being close to home."

I roll over to face him, not believing the monotone drivel that just came out of his mouth. His eyes are closed tight and the pained look on his face brings me to a pause. *What isn't he telling me?* "Baseball?"

He exhales and opens his eyes, staring at those same stars I was looking at before he came in. "I tore my rotator cuff during the playoffs sophomore year," he finally says, shrugging his shoulders.

"Oh, Deck." Baseball had been his dream growing up. His life. His future. He had lived for baseball. I wrap my arm around his body and lay my head on his chest. "I'm so sorry."

"It is what it is. I'm over it. I'm not on the roster anymore, but they still let me travel with the team occasionally—when it doesn't conflict with my classes." He shrugs dismissively, but I know the gesture and the words are bullshit. The Decker I'd known would never be 'over it.' Baseball is his life. Or at least it had been his life. You can't just erase that.

"No, you're not over it...but it's okay if you don't want to talk about it. I understand." And boy do I ever understand.

"I've moved on," he continues. "I changed my degree program from business to exercise science, with a concentration in motor development. I'd like to go into physical therapy. Sports medicine."

I smile, "That's amazing, Deck. You'd be a great therapist." And it would be a great way for him to stay connected to the sport he loves so much.

"Thanks," he says, but it's hollow. His inability to play ball has affected him more than he'll admit, but I know better. I won't push him though. I have no right considering there are things about my life I don't ever plan to share with him.

"How long are you home for?" he asks, effectively changing the subject again.

"I'm not sure. The semester is almost over, but I'm hoping my professors may let me finish my classes remotely. I had only planned a temporary leave before..." I trail off, not wanting to say it out loud. Not wanting to say why my travel plans have changed. "Maybe I can find a local university that would be willing to proctor my exams. I don't know. I just don't want to leave Mom."

"I think that, given the circumstances, and the fact that you're probably still as good a student as you were in high school, they probably won't turn you down."

I nod against his chest, "You're probably right."

"Do you think you'll stay through the summer?" He sounds so hopeful. I wish I could stay the entire summer. Hell, I wish I could manipulate time and make that summer after high school last forever so I could just be with Decker without all the complications that followed after I left town.

"I don't know. I have a job and an apartment back in California. My job will hold my place for a little while, but not forever. And my roommate might get a little lonely if I don't come back." I feel him tense when I mention my roommate.

"I'm sure *she* will be fine." He emphasizes the 'she,' and I realize that he's probing. Is Decker Abrams jealous that I might have a male roommate?

I decide to cater to his unsaid question. "*Kate*, my roommate, probably will be fine." I feel him relax. "But she's my friend, too. We're kind of all each other has out there."

I feel him tense again. "You have people here, too, you know? You always have."

I sigh, "I know." *Not tonight, Deck. Please.*

"Promise me you won't run off without saying goodbye this time."

I blink back the tears I'd thought had run dry. "I promise."

He rolls onto his right side, facing me, and nudges me to roll over as well. Once I'm also on my right side, he pulls my back against his chest again and nuzzles his face between my neck and shoulder. I smile at the familiarity of it all. Decker and I have fallen asleep like this countless times in the past.

It's too easy to fall into a routine with him. Way too easy. I have to watch myself and be extremely careful. I can't put myself, or Decker, in a position where my leaving here will be as painful as it was three years ago.

Because the reality is, I will be leaving again.

Chapter Nine

Casey

The wake and funeral service for my father were the most difficult experiences of my life. Up until that point, I'd thought nothing would beat freshman year of college, but I'd been wrong. Of course, I never thought I'd have to bury my dad. Saying goodbye to my daddy forever was earth-shattering.

My mother and I had held each other on the front bench of the funeral home, then again later at the church. Mr. and Mrs. Abrams were on Mom's left and Decker was on my right, holding us together and providing silent support.

Decker never left my side during the viewing or the funeral, not one time. And his presence had given me strength that I selfishly took. Everyone gathered for a small reception at the Abrams' home after the services. My grandparents had all passed away when I was very young and my parents were only children, so those in attendance were distant aunts, uncles, cousins, and friends of my parents. The few friends I'd had in grade school were away at college, not that I'd kept in touch, so Decker was the only person there for me. He was my person.

I'm sitting on the Abrams' front porch swing, trying to get some fresh air, when Decker joins me. He'd been by my side all day and night like a shadow, a very sweet shadow, I hadn't even realize he'd stepped away. It just goes to show how much of a zone I've been in.

"Here," he says, handing me a red cup filled with a dark liquid. I sniff it; it's wine.

I giggle at the southern stereotype of wine in a red cup. My acquaintances in California would probably pass out from shock if they saw me drinking wine out of anything other than the appropriate glass.

"What's funny?" he asks, sitting down beside me.

"Nothing. There are just some things I miss about home, you know?"

"Actually, no. I don't know. I never really left home." He doesn't say it with an attitude, but it's certainly implied and I grimace. He notices, "I'm sorry, Case."

"No, you should be able to speak your mind, Decker," I tell him.

"Not today of all days." I'm not going to argue with that. But I've been home for three days already, so I know it's only a matter of time before the dam bursts, and he holds nothing back.

The front door opens, and my mom steps outside. "There you are, dear."

"Hey, Mom," I say, standing up.

"I think I'm ready to head home. You sticking around longer?"

I shake my head 'no,' and sneak a quick glance at Decker. He's looking down at his feet. "I'll just see if Mrs. Abrams needs any help with anything before I head out."

Decker stands up and puts his hand on my shoulder. "Don't worry about it, Case. I'll help Mom clean up."

"That's so sweet. Thank you, Decker," my mom tells him. "Always such a sweet boy," she pats him lovingly on the cheek before heading for the steps down to the front yard.

I turn to Decker, "I'd better go."

He raises his hand to my face and brushes his fingers down my cheek. I lean into his chest and he wraps his arms around me, resting his chin on my head. He's about six inches taller than my five-foot-six, the perfect height for this.

"Should I come by later?" he asks quietly. It's almost as if he's waiting for the night when I refuse him.

"Please," I whisper, closing my eyes tight in an effort to block the need from my voice. Three days, and I've already come to rely on him as much as I did in high school.

He kisses the top of my head and then pulls back. "I'll see you later."

I nod in response and hurry down the steps to catch up with my mom, looping my arm through hers.

"You know, Decker can just use the front door."

My heart skips a beat and I stop, jerking her to a stop as well. *What?*

My mom looks over at me and laughs at the shocked expression on my face. "Casey, I may be old, but I'm not stupid. You think I don't know he's been sneaking in your bedroom window for years? Your father threatened to cut down that tree so many times."

"Dad knew?" *Oh my God!* I am completely mortified. "Why didn't y'all ever say anything?

~ 69 ~

How come I was never grounded? Aren't fathers supposed to chase boys away from their daughters with shotguns or something?"

"Casey...you were a straight A student and you never did anything wrong. Jeez, we wanted you to rebel, for crying out loud. To step outside the box and live a little. And you were with Decker. He was a good boy. He *is* a good boy, like a second child to us. Sure you two were sneaking around behind our backs, but you weren't doing anything wrong."

In an instant my shock at this revelation morphs into sadness.

"I'm sorry sweetie, I wasn't thinking." She unloops our arms and puts hers around my shoulder, pulling me in.

"It's okay, Mom. It's just hard is all. Being back...the memories...and dad."

"I know, sweet girl. I wish I could say it'll get easier, but I don't know that it will."

"Time heals all wounds..." I say, repeating what my therapist always tells me.

We approach our front door and Mom turns to me. "What do you say we pig out on some ice cream?"

I smile, "Frozen yogurt?"

"Right," she winks. "Frozen yogurt."

"I'd say you have yourself a deal."

And that's what we do. On the night of my father's funeral, when we're finally alone, my mom and I sit at the bar in the kitchen in our pajamas and scarf down bowl after bowl of frozen yogurt.

And despite my text that he can use the front door, Decker still climbs in my bedroom window.

***

I wake up the next morning to a smiling Decker. At least I think it's morning. I look passed him and note that it's still kind of dark outside. I wipe the sleep from my eyes and glance over at my alarm clock. The green numbers tell me it's just before six.

"There better be a good reason for this," I mutter grumpily.

His smile never falters, "There is. We're going fishing!"

At his announcement, I sit straight up. My smile now matching his. "Well, why didn't you say so?" I haven't been fishing in so long. The last time I'd gone was with my dad and Decker, and I know this is Decker's way of reminding me that I'll keep Dad alive in my memories.

He laughs and raises himself from his squat on the floor beside my bed. "Get dressed, I've got everything loaded into the truck already. We just need to stop for bait."

Letting out an excited squeal, I pop out of bed, run to my dresser, and hope there is something in there that'll still fit. It's been so long since I've been home, I can't even remember what I left behind and I don't think the yoga and lounge pants I'd packed from California will be appropriate.

"It'll be a little chilly on the water, and the bugs might be bitin' in a couple hours, so you'll probably want to wear jeans," Decker offers before he backs out of my room. I hear his footsteps on the stairs and then the silent chatter of him and my mother. I briefly wonder what she's doing up this early, but shake it off and get back to my search.

After settling on a pair of straight-legged jeans I'd had in high school that are a little too big and a cream-colored Columbia fishing shirt, I grab my fishing hat off its hook in my closet and head downstairs. My dad had gotten me the hat when I was twelve. Once upon a time it was a light khaki, now it's darker from years and years of use. There's also a bunch of hand-picked feathery lures around the top. We never fly-fished, but I'd thought they were pretty so my dad hooked me up, literally. I smile at the memory of us in the bait and tackle shop picking out the prettiest lures as I twirl the hat around my fingers.

Arriving in the kitchen, I see my mom bagging up sandwiches while Decker is loading containers into a cooler.

"You were in on this?" I ask my mom, causing them both to look over at me in the doorway.

"Of course," she winks. "Can't have my baby going out on the water without sustenance."

I roll my eyes, "Right. Can't have that." I move over to the cooler to see what's on the menu for the day.

"Don't worry, Case. We weren't plotting behind your back. I just needed your mom's help accessing the boat."

I pause my movements. The boat. Of course we're going out on my dad's boat. Decker doesn't have one, neither does his dad. They always went out on our boat. Why didn't I consider that before now? I guess it was always just a given we'd go out on my dad's boat...even when it was just me and Deck.

"Hey, now," my mom says, stepping over to me and putting her arm around my shoulder. "Your dad would want you two out there on that boat. Nothing would make him happier than seeing it put to use." And seeing me and Decker together again, that's what her eyes are telling me. He never did fully understand why I didn't make amends with Decker, even though he respected my decision.

I nod absently. I know she's right...about all of it. It's just that I have so many memories with Dad on that boat. Some

~ 73 ~

included Decker and his dad, but most were just me and my Dad. I told him about California on that boat. All my hopes and dreams. I haven't even seen it in years. I take a deep breath.

"You okay?" Decker asks, concern etching his features. "We don't have to go on the boat if you don't want to. We can just fish from the dock," he gestures towards the backyard, where a dock stretches out from my backyard to the creek.

"Nonsense," my mother says. "You two are going out on the boat." She gives me a squeeze. "It'll be fun. You'll have fun."

I meet Decker's eyes again, and he gives me a reassuring smile. My mom is right. My trepidation is nonsense. I'd always had fun on that boat and my memories are nothing but positive ones. It's nothing to be scared of.

I smile back at Decker. This would be fun. It's time to make some new memories with Decker.

Chapter Ten

Decker

Casey and I are having a great time so far on the river. We haven't caught anything yet, but we're having some good laughs as we reminisce. I remember the first time we went out on the boat together with our dads when we were seven.

"I'm not touching that!" Casey shrieked.

"It's just a worm," I teased, holding it up to her face.

She backed away from me so quickly that she bumped into my dad, who bumped into her dad, who then fell overboard, headfirst.

Her eyes widened and she brought her hands up to cover her mouth. Her eyes filled with tears as she watched as her dad sputtered up to the surface.

"Daddy! I'm so sorry," she cried.

After my dad helped him back on board, Mr. Evans looked at his little girl with a smile spread from ear to ear.

"It's okay, sugar. Hazards of a small boat is all." Casey's lower lip quivered as big crocodile tears dripped down her cheeks. "Oh, Casey," her dad said, quickly wrapping himself in a towel and bringing her into his arms. "It's okay, sweet girl. Accidents happen."

"It's not her fault," I spoke up. "I put the worm in her face and scared her." Both dads looked over at me, and I shrunk into myself. I was always getting into trouble these days. Just couldn't seem to stay out of trouble—mischief is what my mom called it.

"It's alright, son. No one was hurt," my dad said, patting me on the shoulder. "Just be careful."

After a few more minutes of Mr. Evans calming Casey down, we were back to baiting our hooks.

"I'll bait your hook for you, Casey," I offered.

She shyly handed me her small pink fishing pole. "Thank you, Decker."

"I'm sorry for teasing you," I quietly said as I focused on putting the worm on the hook. I didn't like seeing Casey cry.

"It's okay," she smiled. "Momma says boys only tease girls when they like them. And you're my best friend so you're supposed to like me. So I guess you're supposed to tease me, too."

I wasn't sure what her mom was talking about, but I nodded anyway. Casey was my best friend...and I did like her.

"Whatcha thinking about over there?" she asks me, bringing me back to the present. We had just pulled up to the riverbank for a rest and are settling down on a blanket to start our picnic lunch.

"Just thinking about the first time our dads took us out fishing on the boat."

A sad smile graces her face. "That certainly was memorable," she gently laughs.

"I thought our dads were gonna throw me overboard," I confess.

She full out laughs now; I love that sound. I miss that sound. "Have you met our dads? When would they have ever gotten angry enough to throw one of their kids overboard?"

I laugh with her, "You're right."

"You know," she begins, picking at lint on the blanket, "last night, my mom told me her and my dad knew you used to sneak in my window at night."

My eyes widen and I can feel the blood leave my face.

They knew? How much did they know? Obviously not much since they never bolted the window shut and I'm still alive.

She sees the expression on my face and giggles before looking back down at the invisible lint. "Don't worry, I think our secret's safe. She basically said they were pleased that I was breaking the rules and that we were good kids, so they didn't see the harm."

"Kind of contradicts the whole breaking the rules thing then, doesn't it? If they were okay with it?" I point out.

"Yeah...and the fact that I never really thought I was doing anything wrong. It was always so easy with you, Decker. Everything was so easy back then," she wistfully adds before she looks off at the water.

I want her to tell me more. I want to know everything she felt back then. And everything she feels now. Especially regarding me. But I know this isn't the time to bring it up. Hell, I'm not sure if there will ever be a good time to bring it up. She just seems so fragile, like she's hanging on by a thread...and she might just be.

"Why don't we see what Momma E packed for us?" I say, changing the subject.

Casey turns back to me and smiles, silently thanking me for the distraction from whatever thoughts were running through her head. She reaches over and helps me unload the various containers and baggies.

"Looks like she packed enough for a small village," I say as I pull out a third container of raw vegetables. "And it's all healthy, too." The containers are all filled with various fruits and veggies and the baggies have different kinds of nuts. The sandwiches are turkey and cheese complete with lettuce and tomato. There's even a couple containers of yogurt at the bottom with attached bags of granola.

"Your mom turn into a health nut or something?" I ask as I unload the last of it.

"Or something," Casey says quietly.

Shit. Her mom probably is concerned about eating healthy given what happened to Mr. Evans. Why do I always stick my foot in my mouth?

"It'll get easier, Case." She looks up at me in question. "Him being gone. It'll probably always be difficult, but it'll get easier."

She gives me a small smile and nods. "I'm starved, let's eat."

We're silent for the rest of our time on the riverbank, just eating our lunch and watching the birds fly over the water, occasionally swooping down to catch a fish. They're doing a better job than us. Every now and again I catch these shadows in Casey's eyes, like there is something haunting her. It could just be the guilt of not being with her dad when he passed, but something tells me it's more than that. I just wish she'd trust me enough to let me in. The old Casey did.

***

When we get back, I back into the Evans' driveway so I can return the boat. As we're unloading Casey's gear, my dad walks up.

"Hey, kids, catch anything?" he asks.

"Hey, Mr. Abrams," Casey smiles. "Actually, we did!" She bounces on her toes with her excitement and, for a moment, I catch a glimpse of the girl I used to know.

"Oh yeah?" My dad's whole face lights up. He loves fresh catch. "What've we got?" he asks, rubbing his hands together.

"Drums and bass," I tell him as I pop open the cooler and show him the fish.

"Whoa, you kids did well. I'll fire up the grill," he says and then turns to Casey. "Go get your momma and come on over."

"Okay, but I'm gonna shower first."

"Take your time, darlin'," my dad tells her, and she smiles and waves as she runs off to her house, just like she would have done years ago. Once she's out of earshot, he turns back to me. "How's she doing?"

I shrug, "I don't know, Dad. One minute she's laughing and the next minute it's like she's in another place. She won't really talk to me about anything. Sticks to safe topics like memories or school."

He pats my back, "Just be there for her, son. It's all you can do." He looks back up to the Evans' house, shakes his head, and then looks back at me with a depressing look on his face. "Poor kid. She's had a rough time, Deck. Just be her friend. I think she needs that."

My dad helps me unhitch the boat and then drives my truck back over to the house so he can get started on the fish. I rinse off the boat and think about what he said. *Just be her friend.* When have I ever not been her friend? Why would that ever change? Even when I've been at my angriest with her for leaving, I still would have given anything for just one more minute with her.

***

Dinner is a blast. My dad grilled the fish to perfection and my mom and Mrs. Evans made a green salad and potato salad and Mom fried up some okra and French fries. It's the first time Casey and I have had a cookout together with our parents where we are old enough to have alcohol, and, consequently, the wine and beer are flowing. But it isn't lost on anyone that it's also the first family cookout without Mr. Evans.

We all laugh and share stories. Some are oldies but goodies and others we'd never shared before. I share a few funny stories from some of the road trips I'd taken with the team and Casey shares some of her tales from California. It's obvious that she loves it there, and she's such a great storyteller that I'm at the edge of my seat the entire time she's speaking. Or maybe it's that she's finally speaking freely, and I desperately need to soak it all in.

Either way, the night is perfect.

Chapter Eleven

Casey

A few days after Decker and I went fishing, I wake up alone. I shouldn't be pissed off, but I am. Decker has been spending the night, every night, since I have been home. We spent the days after the fishing trip at the aquarium, the beach, and the Beaufort drive-in. It was all too easy to fall into old habits with him. Nothing has happened between us on a physical level; I won't let it, but every night he holds me until I fall asleep. I should have expected him to eventually fall back into *his* old habit of disappearing before the sun came up.

Waking up in a rotten mood had apparently been a sign of things to come. The rest of my day was crap. While helping my mom box up some of my dad's things to take to the homeless shelter, I get a cardboard paper cut that won't stop bleeding. Then I trip carrying the boxes out to the car and skin both my knees.

What makes it all worse is that I haven't heard a peep from Decker all day. Not. A. Word. His stupid red truck hasn't been in the driveway at all, and I can't help but feel like history is repeating itself.

I'm Decker's convenience friend all over again. Only this time, I'm not putting out, so I guess I can't really be surprised he bailed.

Stupid Decker Abrams.

Which is why later that evening finds me sitting on a wobbly, torn stool at Bill's Tavern, nursing my third Cabernet Sauvignon, which I can no longer pronounce properly and have resorted to calling "cab." This caused a tad bit of confusion with Sam, the bartender, who actually tried to call me a cab when I slurred my last order.

Sam had been one of Decker's good friends growing up. They had been on the baseball team together, but Sam wasn't interested in going pro like Decker had been. His great-granddad was the Bill of 'Bill's Tavern' and he was content carrying on the family tradition behind the bar. Sam had always been nice to me when we were kids. He'd never participated in the endless ribbing I got from the rest of the cool kids. He and Decker were a lot alike.

Decker.

I grunt and down the rest of my wine.

"Want me to call him?" Sam asks.

"Why would I want you to do that?" I slur; even in my slight stupor I know who he's talking about.

Sam leans forward, elbows on the bar and smirks at me. I want to wipe that smirk off his pretty boy face. He has the total beach bum look going on. He's muscular with a dark, too-much-time-on-the-beach tan. Longish blonde hair that's messily styled. And bright blue eyes that are probably that color from spending so much time in the ocean. He's probably full of sea water.

Hey, no one ever said you had to make sense when you were drunk.

"You've been sitting over here mumbling to yourself for the past hour and eighty percent of what comes out of your mouth is 'Decker this' or 'Decker that.' Thought you might just want me to put you out of your misery already."

I scoff. Suddenly I don't like Sam all that much, and I want to punch him right in his smirk. "Yeah, right. I don't want to talk to *Decker.*" I roll my eyes for added effect.

"Look, I don't know what went down with you two after high school–" he starts.

"You're right, you don't," I snap.

He ignores me, "But you should cut him some slack. He was pretty torn up after you left."

"He was torn up? That's rich. Like you said, you don't know shit. Give me more wine." I lift my glass and twirl it by the stem. I know I'm being a bitch, but I don't give a shit right now. Decker wasn't the only victim back then.

"Maybe you should slow it down," Sam says, his eyes darting down to my chest.

I widen my eyes before I quickly tug my V-neck shirt up and narrow my eyes at him in warning. "Maybe you should mind your own damn business."

He raises his hands, palms facing me, and backs away.

"I want another cab!" I shout.

He shakes his head but does as he's told.

"You don't even get what I went through back then. You don't understand." I whine as he places the fresh glass in front of me. Yes, now I am a drunk, emotional girl.

"So why don't you tell me?" he offers as he wipes down the bar top in front of me.

I take my glass and spin the stem between my fingers, looking down at the burgundy liquid. "He broke me, Sam. He broke me in such an agonizingly slow manner. I loved him, you know? More than I should have. More than he loved me."

You're my best friend.

I look up to meet Sam's eyes. They're sad. Full of pity.

Fucking great. More pity. Just what I need.

"Did you ever talk to him about how you felt?"

I can't help it; I start laughing hysterically. "Did I...ever talk...to him...about how I...felt?" I say between giggles.

Sam's looking at me like I've lost my mind. Maybe I have.

"I think he had a pretty good idea of how I felt when he was inside me night after night," I say flatly.

Sam's eyes are wide now. He didn't know? Shocker.

"What? You didn't know? Of course not. Why would you? I was just his dirty little secret. Not good enough to be with in public, but good enough to sneak into my room every night. I lost my virginity to him! I gave everything to him!"

Sam's eyes are darting around the bar, and I look around, noticing that conversations have stopped and people are staring. Whatever. They can stare all they want. I wouldn't be here long enough to give a damn what these people thought of me.

My shoulders slump in defeat. "He never felt that way about me, Sam." I can't stop the tears that build up behind my eyes. "He was just so into himself and his popular friends. He didn't care about me or how I felt. He never even asked me what my plans were after school. I would have told him. If he cared enough to ask. I never hid anything from him...until I did."

I push my still full wine glass away. "Call me a cab, Sam, will you? A real one."

"I got this, Sam," a familiar voice behind me says.

Well, shit.

Chapter Twelve

Decker

I had to run back to school to pick up some of my missed assignments from my professors this morning. I felt guilty for leaving Casey, but she's been through so much and looked so peaceful sleeping. I'd hoped I'd be there and back in no time, before she even woke up maybe, but I had to wait for one of my professors to finish a three-hour seminar.

When I finally arrive home, right away I notice her car is missing. Panic sets in as I run to her house and bang on the front door.

Not again. Please, not again. She wouldn't have gone back to California without telling me...not this time...would she?

When Mrs. Evans opens the door, I don't even give her a chance to say hello. "Where's Casey?"

"Hey, Decker. She just went out for a bit, do you want to come inside?"

"No, ma'am. Do you know where she went?" Surely she can sense my desperation in my jerky movements. I probably reek of it, too.

"She had a pretty rough day. We took care of some of her dad's things. I think she just needed to let off some steam."

"But do you know where she went?" Clearly I'm not above begging.

She shakes her head, "I'm sorry, I don't. Where do you kids go around here to hang out?"

I think about it, maybe a pool hall? But no one goes to a pool hall by themselves. A bar? Does Casey even drink? She had wine after the funeral and when we cooked out the other night. Bill's!

"Thanks, Mrs. Evans!" I call out as I take off for my truck. I jump in and grab my cell phone out of the center console. I quickly ask Siri for the number to Bill's Tavern, knowing my high school buddy Sam tends bar there a few nights a week. I hope tonight is one of those nights.

"Bill's Tavern."

Thank Christ. "Sam? It's Decker."

He exhales. "It's about damn time. She's here. Better hurry up."

"Why? What's wrong?"

"Nothing...yet. But she's well on her way to being hammered."

"Shit. Thanks, Sam." I hang up the phone and peel out of the driveway, barely checking my rear view mirror for cars or pedestrians.

Chill out, Abrams. Sam's looking out for her. She's not alone. No need to kill yourself or someone else. But why the hell did he let her drink so much?

I ease the truck intro drive and try to go the speed limit all the way to the bar. But let's be honest here, five miles over the limit isn't really speeding, is it?

I pull into the parking lot to Bill's Tavern and cut the engine, breathing a sigh of relief when I see her car parked two spaces over. I take a deep breath and get out of the car, not knowing what I'm about to walk into. I've never seen Casey drunk before. She never used to drink at parties in high school. Hell, she never went to parties in high school. And she's only had a glass or two of wine since I've been home.

I push open the door to the bar, and what I hear completely stops me in my tracks.

"What? You didn't know? Of course not. Why would you? I was just his dirty little secret. Not good enough to be with in public, but good enough to sneak into my room every night. I lost my virginity to him! I gave everything to him!"

The entire place is silent, I swear you can hear the crickets and frogs outside. Sam's wide eyes search the bar, finally landing on mine. Casey, swaying on her bar stool, looks around briefly, not noticing me in the doorway.

"He never felt that way about me, Sam." She continues quietly, slumped down on her stool now. I walk up behind her, ready to catch her if she falls. "He was just so into himself and his popular friends. He didn't care about me or how I felt. He never even asked me what my plans were after school. I would have told him. If he cared enough to ask. I never hid anything from him...until I did."

My heart breaks. That's how she felt...like she was my dirty little secret? That's not true at all. I loved her. I always tried to protect her...to take care of her. Hell, I didn't think I deserved her. She was so much better than I was. Had I really come off as being that selfish back then? And that's the reason she didn't tell me she was leaving? Because she didn't think I cared?

She pushes her full glass towards Sam. "Call me a cab, Sam, will you?"

"I got this, Sam," I tell him, breaking my silence and causing Casey to startle.

She slowly turns to face me, and I see the wet streaks on her cheeks from her tears. I did this to her. I broke my best friend. Or rather a major miscommunication did. But yeah...it's mostly my fault.

"Come on," I tell her, reaching for her hand. "Let's get you home."

She swats my hand away. "I don't want to go home with you!" she screams, attracting more attention than she already had.

I know she's pissed at me and I get it. I really do. But drunk or not, pissed off or not, I'm not going to put up with her shit. I close my eyes and pinch the bridge of my nose.

"Casey, get up," I tell her firmly, looking directly into her eyes now.

"No," she says, crossing her arms over her chest defiantly.

I sigh. "Then I'm gonna have to do this the hard way."

She looks at me with confusion before her face fills with shock as I bend over and press my shoulder into her stomach, lifting her up and onto my shoulder. Thankfully she's wearing shorts so she's not giving anyone a show. Well, any more of a show than her

~ 93 ~

beating on my back and screaming like a banshee.

"Put me down, Decker Oscar Abrams!"

I nod at Sam, who mouths "Oscar" at me. Yeah, I'm never going to live that down now. Thank you, Casey.

"I am *so* telling your mother!"

"Go ahead, princess. Tell her all about how you were running your mouth in the bar and being a brat when I offered to see that you got home safely. While you're at it, tell your mom, too. Take out an announcement in the paper for all I care."

She slumps in defeat, making it much easier for me to carry her. "I hate you."

"No, you don't." I say, though I'm not really sure if that's true after what I heard a few minutes ago. I set her down on her feet just outside my truck. "You know we're going to talk about this, don't you?"

She rolls her eyes. "Whatever."

I open the passenger door and give her a boost up. She swats at me twice while I'm trying to help her buckle her seatbelt, and I want to laugh, but I know that won't help things any. I shut her door, walk around the front of the truck, and get in.

"I'm sorry you heard all that," she tells me quietly. Her head is now lying back on the headrest and her eyes are closed. I bet she'll be asleep before we even get out of the parking lot.

"It's how you feel. Don't be sorry for how you feel." Even if I can't stand the thought of her feeling that way towards me. Especially when she doesn't know the whole truth.

"I was just so mad at you, Decker," she breathes out.

"I know, Casey. And we'll talk about it. But not tonight."

"Not tonight," she repeats.

I start the truck and head home. Sure enough, she's asleep before we pull out onto the main road. I can't believe that all this time I've been mad at her, she's been mad at me. If we'd just talked back then, really talked about shit instead of dancing around the real stuff, maybe the past three years wouldn't have happened. At least not like they did. Maybe I'd still have my best friend and wouldn't be terrified I was going to lose her.

As I'm taking the turns through our neighborhood, admittedly a little faster than I normally would since there aren't any cars on the road, Casey groans. "Imgonnabesick," she garbles before leaning forward and puking all over her legs, the car seat, and the floorboards of my truck.

Fantastic.

The perfect end to the perfect night.

Not.

Chapter Thirteen

Casey

The following morning, I wake up feeling like absolute shit. To make matters worse, my mother is sitting beside my bed when I finally open my eyes. I can't decipher the look on her face through the haze surrounding my brain, and I don't even want to. I know what I'll see if I take the time to focus. Disappointment.

"Take this," she snaps, roughly handing me a couple white pills and a glass of water.

I lift myself up on my elbows, wincing at the sunlight pouring in the room through the open blinds. I drop the pills on my tongue and swallow them down with the water. Glancing over at my nightstand I take note of the bottled vitamin drink, toast, and assortment of other pills. I set the water glass down and flop back into the mattress; the movement causes my stomach to turn, and I groan.

"What the hell were you thinking?" my mother hisses at me, obviously through with the silence.

My eyes pop open. She's mad at me?

"I am so *disappointed* in you, Casey." Ah, there it is.

"I'm sorry, mom. I won't do it again," I drone monotonously, pinching my eyes tightly shut again in an effort to block the sunshine.

"Do you have any idea what could have happened to you?" Clearly, she's not finished with her lecture. She's never had to do this to me before, so I guess I should be a little more patient and understanding.

"I'm fine," I tell her, making eye contact this time. "See? I'm right here. I'm in one piece."

"Casey...I know the last few years have been rough and you never really acted like a kid even before that. But there is no reason to catch up on all that you missed in one night."

"Mom, I had a few glasses of wine. That's it. I drink wine in California. I'm of age, it's not that big a deal."

She shakes her head. "You have to be more careful than that. I already lost my husband..." her voice breaks. "I refuse to lose my daughter, too."

I sigh, taking her hand in mine and using my other hand to rub her back as she quietly sobs at my bedside. I wish I could promise her she'll never lose me, I wish I could alleviate that concern...but it's inevitable, right?

**

Mom and I had a heart-to-heart and I promised her I wouldn't drink excessively again. I even offered to not touch alcohol all together if it made her feel better, but she insisted it was fine in moderation. My promise certainly wouldn't solve all our problems, but it's a start. One tiny victory that made my mom feel better, that's what was important. After she had finally calmed down, I retreated to one of my most favorite places. The dock in our backyard.

Apparently I had slept most of the day away because it's already dusk. The sky is painted gorgeous shades of blue and orange. Blended together it looks like a brilliant abstract painting. I miss the Carolina night sky; California sunsets are different. I take a seat at the end of the dock, not quite far enough for my legs to bend over the edge—it's still too cold for that—but my heels are lined up perfectly with the last wooden plank.

Snippets of last night start making their way back to me. I can't believe Decker heard those things I'd said about him. About us. And hell, I can't even believe I said those things! Poor Sam. He probably hadn't been expecting all that when he took my drink order. He's a bartender, so I suppose it's not the worse he's ever heard...but still, he and Decker were good friends and it was so inappropriate for me to unload on him like that. I'll have to apologize to him before I leave town.

The boards behind me bump and creak as footsteps approach. I don't even have to turn around to know it's him. It's Decker. He stops right behind me and sits down, legs spread on either side of my body. I bend my knees and press myself back against his chest. I can't not do it...it's reflexive, even after all these years. He continues our old routine by wrapping his arms around me and pulling me in snug, resting his head on my shoulder, the side of his face against the side of mine.

I don't know what to say to him but I know I need to say something. I at least owe him *some* explanation after what he walked in on last night. But where do I even begin? I'm not even sure how much of my little outburst he'd heard. But regardless...I'd blindsided him.

"I had no idea you felt that way," he finally says, breaking the peaceful silence.

"I'm sorry, Decker." Not knowing which part he's talking about. The part where I'd said I loved him or about how angry I'd been with him. Well, I know he at least heard that part.

"Don't be sorry. It's how you felt. How you feel."

"I'm not apologizing for my feelings, just my delivery." And that's the truth. I will always love Decker. He'll always be my first love and my best friend. I'll never apologize for that. And I'm not pissed at him anymore—I had forgiven him for everything the moment I'd arrived in California alone. Hell, I forgave him before I even crossed the first state line.

He chuckles. "Roger that. I just wish you would have told me you were upset with me. You never held that shit back, Case. I knew something was up with you that summer, but I figured if you were mad at me, you would have given me hell. You never let things like that fester." So he must not have heard the love stuff. He would have been all over that if he had. It's so much better that he hadn't heard that part.

I sigh. "I was trying to make sense of everything. Part of me knew I was more to you than all that. More to you than anyone else was. But the teenage girl part of me...she was so mad at you, Deck. She didn't understand why it seemed you had two lives...one with her and one with everyone else."

He's quiet for a moment, then speaks. "I always wanted to protect you, Case. You were so innocent and unassuming."

"Are you suggesting I was naïve?" I ask, stiffening in his arms.

"No, not at all. You've always been the smartest person I know. Even at college, I still haven't met anyone as smart as you. And you aren't just book smart either, you're street smart, too. Maybe not bar smart, though," he adds with a chuckle, trying to lighten the mood I'm sure.

I laugh with him. "Maybe not."

"I just wanted to have something that was all my own. You were mine. Just mine." Tingles run through all the important parts of my body when he says that. *Mine*. I wish I would have looked at it that way back then. I wish he would have *claimed* me like that back then. Might have made a difference.

"You never did share well with others." I feel his smirk against my cheek.

"No, I never did." He takes a deep, heavy breath. "My friends in high school were all immature, Case. You know that. I didn't want you around the stupid shit they'd do. You were so good, so pure...they were always getting into trouble and just barely getting out of it because of their status on whatever team they belonged to. I didn't want all that to taint you. You were just too good for all that."

I hadn't thought of it like that...I hadn't thought of it from Decker's perspective at all really. He had to have known from the handful of times I did go out with his jock friends that I wasn't enjoying myself and that their behavior was a complete turn off for me from a fun standpoint. And the girls...don't even get me started. I guess I can sort of understand why he wouldn't want me around them. Aside from the graduation party, he never once invited me out with his friends. He could have at least asked. That's what hurt my feelings. I feel like he hid what we were doing from everyone. Like he was ashamed. Sure we'd never talked about what we were to each other, aside from best friends...but still...was he just that insensitive to the wants and needs of women? Was I expecting too much?

We sit in silence for a few moments and, despite the knot in my stomach from my wayward thoughts, it's a comfortable silence. It's always been this way with Decker. When we were little and I was mad at him for stealing or breaking one of my toys, I was still so comfortable in his presence. I've missed that the past three years.

"I was so mad at you for leaving," he suddenly says. "I think I actually hated you for a week."

"Just a week?" I try to joke and fail.

He keeps speaking as though he wasn't interrupted. "We were best friends. Spent every day together, most nights. We spent the night together and then you were just gone."

Well *that's* not exactly fair. He was gone first. He just up and left, like he always had. Ran off to do whatever with whomever.

"Well maybe if you were around in the morning, I would have said goodbye," I snap.

He sighs. "I don't want to fight with you, Casey. I just want to understand what happened. I know something was up with you all summer, and I was trying to give you time to tell me, but you never did. And then I had to find out like that. In a bar. With an audience. It just doesn't seem right."

"We made mistakes, Deck. Things probably would have been fine if we had stayed just best friends, but we blurred the lines."

"Seems like we're always blurring the lines," he says, squeezing me between his arms for emphasis.

"Seems we are," I whisper.

There's a sudden change in the air as Decker nuzzles my cheek with his nose. Our breaths are heavier. His hands wander down my arms. Goosebumps prickle up and down my arms.

No. No, no, no.

This is *not* okay. This is *not* good. This can*not* happen.

I quickly break free of his hold and jump to my feet, nearly falling into the water in the process.

"I'm leaving tomorrow," I blurt, facing away from him.

I hadn't planned on leaving, but I have to. I can't go through this again with him. Not now. If I stay, the lines will continue to blur and we'll fall back into the destructive pattern we started four years ago when we shared our first kiss...right here on this dock.

There wasn't a cloud in the sky and the stars twinkled brightly, despite the bright moonlight nearly drowning them out. The water gently flowed by in the creek and the crickets chirped, providing the perfect soundtrack and the perfect backdrop to our night.

Our parents were out of town at a banquet; they'd be out all night, trusting Decker and I to keep each other company and to keep each other safe for the evening. Sleepovers between Decker and I weren't uncommon, and there was never any reason for our parents to think it was inappropriate. We were best friends from the age of six, practically raised as siblings.

Decker and I crept out onto the dock with some candles and a bottle of wine we stole from his parents' wine cellar. They had seven of the same bottle so we figured they wouldn't miss this one.

Things recently changed between me and Decker. He'd started looking at me differently.

I know I grew boobs and all, but I still played baseball like the best of them. He didn't like it when other guys talked to me at school and told them to back off. But he wouldn't talk to me at school like they did, either. I didn't think it was fair, but Decker said he'd always look out for me so I just had to assume he knew something about those guys that I didn't.

"Have you kissed anyone, Casey?" Decker asked after we spread out the blanket and sat down cross-legged at the end of the dock.

I laughed. "No, Deck. Guys don't want to kiss me."

"That's not true," he said.

"Then how come I'm seventeen and I've never been kissed?"

He looked down at his hands, fidgeting in his lap.

"Decker?" I asked sternly. *What did he do?*

"I may have threatened a few of the guys on the team."

"What?! Why? How?" I couldn't believe he did that. *No wonder guys never talked to me, let alone kissed me. I knew I was plain and all, but still. There's someone for everyone, right? All those guys that talked to me and he chased away...*

"None of those guys are good enough for you."

"Shouldn't that be for me to decide?" I cross my arms over my chest, downright pissed off now.

How dare he?

"I'm sorry, Case."

"Hmmf." I stared off into the water, ignoring him.

Decker sighed. "You know what? I'm not sorry. I don't want you kissing other guys and that's that."

My eyes snapped back to his. "Excuse me?"

"You heard me," he said, looking down at his hands again.

"Yeah, I heard you. That's a bunch of crap, Decker. You can't just run interference all my life." If I wasn't sitting, I would have stomped my feet.

"Wanna bet?"

I rolled my eyes. Arguing with him was useless. He was the most stubborn person I knew, next to myself of course.

"Whatever, Decker."

He sighed again. "I want to be your first kiss," he whispered, so quietly I barely heard him.

"What did you just say?"

He looked up at me. "I said I want to be your first kiss."

"What? Why? Decker?" I didn't know what to say. Where was this coming from? Decker wants to kiss me? Why?

"Because when I think back to my first kiss, I want it to be a happy memory. And Casey, all my memories with you are happy ones."

I felt tears well up in my eyes. Well, if that wasn't the sweetest thing Decker Abrams had ever said to me. And I'd be his first kiss, too? Gorgeous Decker Abrams has never kissed a girl?

He groaned at the tears. "Don't cry, Case."

"Happy tears, Deck. Happy tears," I smiled at him.

He grinned that boyish grin I loved so much that always got him out of trouble...with me and every other female in his life.

"So you've really never kissed a girl before?" I still found that hard to believe, but Decker had never lied to me before.

He shook his head. "No. I wanted it to be special, you know?"

I nodded, "Yeah, I know."

"So can I?" he asked, scooting closer to me on the blanket.

"Can you what?" He moved even closer.

"Kiss you?" I could feel his breath on my face, he was so close.

"Please," I whispered, closing my eyes.

His lips brushed mine and I felt tingles all over my body. His lips were so soft, yet so firm. Suddenly his tongue was pressed against the seam of my lips. It was such a strange sensation. I wasn't sure what I was supposed to do, but I wanted to taste him, too.

I opened my mouth and our tongues danced against one another. Touching and twisting, each sampling what the other had to offer. He finally put his arms around me and pulled me close to him. The kiss was amazing and seemingly never-ending, despite the awkward position we were twisted into. He eventually ended it with three short pecks on my lips.

As he pulled away we both opened our eyes. He smiled, so did I.

"Wow," I said.

"Wow," he agreed.

"Can we do that again?" I asked.

"Definitely," he wasted no time, leaning in again.

Decker and I made out under the stars for hours that night. Never letting the other get too far away.

It was the start of something beautiful.

But it was also the beginning of the end.

"You're what?" Decker shouts.

Shit.

Chapter Fourteen

Decker

I can't even believe this shit. She's leaving?
Just like that. Again?!

"Talk to me, dammit!" I yell, jumping to my
feet. She's just standing there with her back
to me, looking out at the water as if she didn't
just destroy my world a second time. I'm so
pissed off right now I just want to push her
off the damn dock. Wouldn't be the first time
either, so she shouldn't test me.

"I'm sorry, Decker. I have finals…"

"That's bullshit," I interrupt. "You said you
were going to arrange to take your finals
here."

"Well, I couldn't make the arrangements. I need to get back or I'll flunk."

She's lying. I know she's lying because she won't face me. Casey has a big thing about eye contact. And she's never this emotionless...never this detached. What the hell is going on?

"Bullshit," I spit out.

She whips around to face me. Finally. "Excuse me?"

"You heard me. I call bullshit." I cross my arms over my chest, matching her stance.

"Ha...right...whatever. That just changes everything. Decker calls bullshit." She shakes her head, sarcastically laughs, and makes a face like I'm the crazy one, meanwhile she's the one stammering.

Casey Evans never stammers. She's the most certain person I know. The most confident. At least she used to be.

"What's all this about?" I ask, gesturing to her defensive stance and attitude. "I thought we were fixing things."

"Right, 'fixing things.'" She mocks, complete with air quotes and eye rolls.

What the fuck? Pushing her in that water is looking better and better. I take a step closer.

"Casey, I don't know what is going through your head right now because I can't read your

~ 112 ~

crazy-ass mind, but you'd better start talking."

Up until that very moment, I had not been aware skin could turn that shade of red.

"I'm sorry, Case," I say, raising my hands in surrender as I try to backpedal—and back step—but it doesn't appear to be working. She still hasn't said a thing, and I swear I can see the heat waves surrounding her head. "I didn't mean to call you crazy."

"I have to go pack," she simply says. I'd wanted her to calm down, but she's suddenly a little bit too calm. Like a veil just dropped over her entire self.

"No, please no. Please don't go, Casey." I consider myself to be pretty manly, but damn if there aren't tears welling up behind my eyes at the thought of her leaving again. Because this time, I don't think she's going to come back. If she leaves now, I'm going to lose her forever. I can feel it. I'm not afraid to beg my long lost best friend to stay. I'm not above anything right about now.

"I have to," she says as she hurries passed me. If I'm not mistaken, there are tears in her eyes, too.

"Casey, please!" I call out, trying to grab hold of her before she's out of reach. I miss.

She briefly pauses at the end of the dock. Without turning around, she says "Goodbye, Decker."

I watch her run across the grass and into the back door of her house. She doesn't look back once. Through the second story window, I see the soft glow of her bedroom light as it turns on, and her figure approaches the glass. She seems startled to see me still standing on the dock, even though it's only been a minute since she left me here. While holding my eyes, she raises her hand and locks the window. Then she closes the blinds.

And just like that, she's gone. Out of my sight.

But not for long...

***

"You sure about this?"

I look up at Sam as I close the lid of my laptop. "More sure than I've ever been in my life."

"For the record, I think you're crazy." I'm not surprised he feels that way. Sam did have a front row seat to Casey's "Decker Bash."

"I don't know what else to do," I say, running my hands through my hair in frustration.

"How about nothing? You've been fine the past two years. After that first year, you got past it. Why go down that road again? The girl's clearly got some baggage and she's really pissed at you."

I shoot him a glare. He's starting to piss me off.

He rolls his eyes in response, "Whatever, dude. Your funeral."

He's probably right. Casey is going to kill me.

I had watched from the living room window as her car pulled away from her house this morning. Her mother had looked completely devastated. The Casey I used to know never would have left her mom like that. High school Casey would have stayed with her mom all summer after losing her dad. Shit, high school Casey would have come home more than once in three years. I don't know what her deal is—it can't *all* be due to me and our fucked up relationship—but I'm going to find out.

Spending time with her again after all these years...it felt like old times. Having the chance to hold her in my arms again ignited something within me. I don't exactly know what it was—maybe love? All things with Casey are practically impossible to define. But it felt good. And now...now I just feel empty. I miss her. I held her not fifteen hours ago, and I already miss her. I thought I had my best friend back. I couldn't have been more wrong.

For the past twenty-four hours or so, all I've replayed in my mind is those words she'd said at the bar. I should have done a better job of showing her how much I valued our friendship in high school. It makes me sick to know she thinks—thought—I'd been using her. It was far from it. She was my best friend, and I just wanted to be with her. I wanted every experience I ever had to be with her. Just like our first kiss and all the intimate moments that followed.

She didn't like the popular crowd, so I thought I was doing her a favor by not inviting her out with my other friends. She was too smart for them, too good for them. They did stupid high school shit, and Casey was so high above all that. She'd thought I believed she wasn't good enough for me? How about the truth...I wasn't good enough for her. No one was good enough for her. It's like that Tal Bachman song, "She's So High."

Maybe if I'd just made the effort to make her feel included and allowed her to decide whether or not to go out with me and my friends...maybe that would have made all the difference. But now I'll never know because the damage has already been done. If I could write a letter to my seventeen year old self...

I'm such a fuck up. First Casey, then my shoulder, now Casey again...

But that's about to change. What Casey Evans doesn't know is that I'm not letting her get away easily this time. I'm going to bust my ass to right all the wrongs I did. I can't go back in time, but I can prove to her that she means as much to me as I do to her. Or as much as I'd meant to her once...I don't even know how she feels towards me anymore.

There's only one way to find out...

Chapter Fifteen

Casey

Pulling into my apartment complex, I am totally, utterly, and completely exhausted. How I made it the last hundred miles will forever escape me. I basically drove straight through from Charleston to Stanford, stopping only for two hour naps here and there along the way. Granted, not the safest thing to do, especially when travelling alone, but I just needed to get the hell out of there and away from Decker. The terrible thing? I already miss him like I imagine one would miss an amputated limb. Only a few days together and it felt like we were never apart.

I left Charleston Saturday morning, and here I am, early Monday afternoon. Burnt out. Worn out. Exhausted. The normally seventy-two hour trip, which includes the gas, food, and lodging stops, took about fifty-five. My dad would have been proud of my time, but pissed off at the danger I put myself in. Lord help me if my mother finds out. I'll have to call her tomorrow to officially let her know I'm home.

I feel bad about leaving her so abruptly. She'd been very upset, but believed the same lie I'd told Decker—I had to get back for finals. The truth is, my professors gave me my leave and sent me take-home finals. I am an excellent student, and they did it without question. Now I'd be completing them from California instead of South Carolina. I'd be a fool not to take advantage of this small luxury I'd been given.

I get out of my car and grab my lone bag off the backseat. I can't wait to take a hot shower to wash the travel off of me, and then fall face-down onto my mattress. My body is sore in places I didn't know existed. As much as I love my roommate, Kate, I really hope she isn't home. If she is home, she'll want to talk about the trip and about my dad. She also knows all about Decker and can read me like a book. I'm not ready to deal with any of that.

I fumble with my purse as I try to locate the key to my apartment, slowly make my way up the outdoor stairs to the third-floor. Fortunately it's in the mid-60s and there is a light breeze, so I'm not sweating from the overexertion. If this was Charleston, I'd be dripping. I guess the fact that I seem to be moving at a pace of five steps per hour helps with that, too.

"Where the *fuck* is it?" I complain. I just had my damn keys at the car. It's amazing how quickly something can get lost in a purse, even a tiny one like mine. "Ah-ha, gotcha sucker," I say, smiling in victory as I spot the pink initialed keychain and yank them from the bottom of my bag with such force that I end up tossing them a few feet in front of me.

"Son of a bitch." My shoulders slump, and I just stand there staring at the keys on the ground. I give up. I've had an emotional week and a long drive and I'm so damn tired and hungry that I just want to cry. Why can't one thing go right? Something as simple as keys? Why?

"I don't remember you having such a foul mouth. That must be a characteristic of California Casey."

I look up at the sound of the voice I've known my entire life...and promptly burst into tears. Not just a few tears streaking down my face, but a drop everything I'm holding, all out sob-fest. Decker approaches me like one would a wounded animal, his hands out in front of him in a gesture of peace. It makes me cry harder, close to the point of hyperventilation.

I want to hit him. *What the hell is he doing here?* But when he pulls me into his chest and wraps his arms around me, I melt. Damn traitorous body, mind, and soul. It knows what I need even when I refuse to acknowledge it. Decker seems to know what I need, too. After a few minutes in his arms, I calm down enough that he lets me go, holding me at arm's length.

"You okay?" he asks, leaning down a little to look in my eyes.

Lost in his beautiful green orbs, I shrug. Am I okay? Hell if I know.

"Why are you here?" I wonder, half-concerned that I'm having a hallucination or still asleep at a rest stop somewhere.

He lets go of my arms and takes a cautious step back. "I let you get away three years ago, Casey. I'm not going to let you get away again."

"Why?" I ask him. I've got no fight in me at the moment—I'm that exhausted. I know I can't really deal with his presence right now, but he's *Decker*.

He blows out a breath, puffing his cheeks out in the process. It's cute. It reminds me of him as a child with his round face and chubby cheeks.

"Because you're my best friend." I roll my eyes, and he steps forward with his hands out in a placating gesture. "But not just that, you're everything to me. You always have been. I did a shit job of showing you that in the past, but I'm going to prove it to you now."

Those are words that would have made me melt three years ago. They would have made me cancel all my plans for Stanford and transfer colleges. I would have stayed home and gone to community college if he had told me that back then.

But now?

Now things have changed.

Now those words hurt.

"It's too late for that, Decker."

"It's not too late, Casey. It's never too late," he argues.

I shake my head. I can't go down this road with him. Not again. This is why I left. This is why I stayed away. I can't do this with him. I'm too damn tired. I'm running on empty.

"I'm sorry, Decker. It's the way it has to be." I pick up my purse and backpack from where I dropped them on the floor, then step around Decker to pick up my keys.

"Casey, we can talk about this," he says firmly.

I put on my best "I mean business" look, which only works to a certain degree when I have the remnants of an ugly cry left on my face, and turn to face him. "There's nothing left to talk about. Go home, Decker." There's no emotion in my voice, my physical and mental exhaustion have seen to that.

He glares right back at me, but doesn't back down. I finally turn from him and walk over to my apartment door, sticking the key in the lock. As I turn the knob and push open the door, he speaks.

"This isn't over. I'm not going anywhere, Casey."

I close my eyes and sigh as I lean my forehead against the apartment door. I know he's not going give up. Decker Abrams never gives up.

***

It's been six hours since I left Decker standing outside the apartment. After practically slamming the door in his face, I did what I had planned to do. I took a long, hot shower, snacked on some cold veggies and dip Kate had in the fridge, and face-planted onto my bed. I slept for a solid five hours, waking up only when I heard the front door shut.

"Case?" Kate's sweet voice calls out. I hear her footsteps on the hardwood floor as she approaches my bedroom.

Kate is great. We were paired with each other in the dorms freshman year and have been inseparable ever since. She's my best friend in California, my only friend really. We each have acquaintances, most of them mutual, but we're both pretty much homebodies and dedicated to our studies, so we don't go out much. She's sort of estranged from her family—her parents are rich snobs, always jet setting somewhere—so she doesn't go home for breaks either. Coincidentally, she's also from South Carolina—Columbia—so we've got that in common. It's like we were meant to find each other here. Two Carolina Girls in the Golden State.

My bedroom door pops open and Kate pokes her head in, her dirty blonde hair in ringlets all around her face.

"You cut your hair?" is the first thing that comes out of my mouth. Before I left, her hair was as long as mine—mid-back. I was only gone for a little more than a week, though realistically I know it takes less than an hour to get a haircut.

"Yeah," she says, stepping into my room. "You like?" she raises her hand to her hair in a self-conscious gesture.

I sit up and cock my head to the side, fully taking in the new style. "I love it. It really suits you," I tell her and mean it. She looks really good. The cut really emphasizes her natural curls and the way it frames her face enhances her high cheekbones.

She smiles, "Thanks." She drops her hand and sits at the end of my bed. "So what are you doing home? Your last text said you were going to stay in South Carolina for a while."

I flop back down on my back, close my eyes, and groan in frustration.

"That good, huh?" she giggles. Kate is a quiet person, very shy. She doesn't laugh out loud, only giggles these sweet little giggles that sound like bells.

I say one word: "Decker." Kate knows all about my history with Decker. She held my hand as I cried one particularly emotional day freshman year, and the whole story came out. That was a day I'd like to forget, and unfortunately one that I'll most likely remember forever.

"Which reminds me," she starts. "Are you responsible for that hunk of man candy snoozing outside the apartment door? Or do I need to call security?"

My eyes open wide and I sit straight up. I'm not sure if I'm more surprised that Decker is sleeping in the breezeway, or that Kate just called him "man candy." So out of character. Kate never refers to men that way. She never refers to men period. In the beginning I wondered if it was because she was interested in women, but that turned out to be false, and a completely embarrassing conversation for both of us.

Focus Casey! Decker is outside the apartment!

I jump out of bed and run to the front door, Kate right on my heels. I swing open the front door and look down. Sure enough, there he is, sleeping like a baby, using his duffel bag as a pillow.

"Decker!" I whisper-shout, nudging him with my foot. "Get up!"

I catch Kate's wide-eyed look out of the corner of my eye as Decker rouses from his slumber. He looks completely disoriented, like he has no idea where he is, and keeps using his fists to rub his eyes. He finally spots me and his face breaks out in his beautiful, heart-stopping smile.

"Hey, Case. What time is it?" His voice is thick with sleep and sexy as hell. I hate him.

"It's time for you to go home! What part of that didn't you understand before?"

"My home is wherever you are," he says, not dropping the smile from his face. Of course he has to be charming. Now. After all this time.

Kate sighs, and I turn to glare at her, raising my eyebrows in a "what the hell?" gesture. She shrugs in response. Again, what the hell? I swear my roommate has been compromised by an alien force. Or she got laid, but in this circumstance, the alien force is a more likely scenario.

When I look back to Decker, I see he's standing now, brushing the grit off his clothes from lying on the dirty concrete.

"Aren't you going to introduce me?" he asks, gesturing to Kate.

I groan, realizing Decker clearly isn't going anywhere. He's going to stick around until he gets whatever it is he came here for.

"Decker, this is my roommate Kate. Kate, this is Decker." They both smile winning smiles and shake hands.

I shake my head and go back inside. I think I need to go back to sleep. Or maybe I *am* still asleep and this is just a dream. Decker isn't still here. Kate hasn't been invaded. And I am going to wake up any minute feeling rested and ready to tackle a new day.

Chapter Sixteen

Decker

Casey's roommate, who I know to be Kate from Casey's stories, introduces herself and invites me into the apartment after Casey had stomped off. Kate's a sweet girl. She seems pretty put together, a lot like Casey, which makes me feel better considering they have been rooming together since freshman year. I'm glad she wasn't paired up with a nut job like I was.

My freshman year I'd roomed with another guy from the baseball team. They kept the jocks together by sport since we had to arrive to campus early and kept the same insane schedules—early mornings and the occasional late nights when traveling for games. My roommate back then, John Lechance, was a junior. Usually they don't pair upperclassmen with lowerclassmen, but they had a hard time placing John, so they stuck him with me. It hadn't taken me long to figure out why. The guy was a loose cannon. I gave him the benefit of the doubt as long as I could, but when I discovered he was using steroids, I drew the line. No way was I going to be around that shit. I made it playing ball on the college level without using performance enhancing drugs; I wasn't about to risk being accused of using because my stupid roommate was. I told Coach; there was an investigation, and John was kicked off the team and expelled from the school. My double was a single for the rest of the year, and I was paired up with someone much cooler sophomore year.

The front door opens right into the living room, and I take a look around as I step inside. It's modestly decorated, with a cream-colored sofa and loveseat and dark wood coffee and end tables. The apartment is an open floor plan, with the kitchen and dining area on one side and sliding doors leading out to the balcony on the opposite side. Abstract paintings hang on the wall behind the television, and picture frames dot the wall behind the couch.

I start to follow Kate to the kitchen, where Casey is sitting at the table with her head in her hands—undoubtedly frustrated beyond belief that I'm still here—but one of the framed photos on the wall catches my eye. I'd recognize that picture anywhere. I have one copy framed in my room at home and another stuck to my pin board in my dorm room.

The picture is of me and Casey on our seventh birthday, blowing out the candles on our joint birthday cake. I remember clearly how I wanted an *Iron Giant* theme and she wanted a *Fantasia* theme. Our moms settled it for us and chose a *Toy Story* theme with both Woody and Jessie. It was the first of many birthdays we had spent together growing up, and the first of many where our parents had to intervene and force a compromise. In fact, we never missed one until college. I thought about her on that first birthday away when all my teammates were going out with their dates for Valentine's Day. I hadn't asked anyone out, not that there weren't any possibilities. I just couldn't stomach the idea of spending even a moment of that day with some meaningless chick. That had always been my day with Casey. I thought about her the two birthdays after that, too. How could I not?

Shaking off the feeling of nostalgia, I walk into the kitchen and take a seat at the table across from Casey. She peeks at me between her fingers, and I grin at her attempt to glare. She's so damn adorable when she's mad.

"I thought I told you to leave," she says, though it's muffled through the hands she still hasn't removed from her face.

"Kate let me in."

"I need a new roommate," she grumbles.

I laugh. "I think she's great."

Casey removes her hands from her face and full on glares at me. She's getting really good at that. "Seriously, Decker. What. Are. You. Doing. Here?" She enunciates each word as if I don't understand English.

"I told you. You mean the world to me, Case. I'm here to prove it to you. I'm not going anywhere, so you'd better get used to it." Her expression shifts slightly at my words and I have a glimmer of hope, but, just as quick as it had appeared, she's back to glaring at me.

"You have finals."

"I made arrangements." I raise my eyebrow at her in challenge.

Her eyes narrow. "I don't want you here."

"Yes, you do. You just don't know it yet."

"Dammit, Decker!" she raises her voice and smacks her hands on the table. "This is my life. You're not a part of it anymore."

Her words hurt, but I know she's only saying what she's saying because she's trying to push me away. She's hiding something. I can feel it. I spent most of the flight here analyzing her behavior when she'd been home. There wasn't anything telling, but something was off...not quite right. And I'm determined to find out what it is.

"Casey, we became best friends when you shared your cookies with me."

From somewhere behind me, I hear what sounds like choking. Casey rolls her eyes, leans to the left to see behind me and calls out, "Not those kinds of cookies, you pervert! What the *hell* did you do with my roommate?"

"Sorry," Kate's quiet voice calls out.

"I thought Kate was your roommate," I ask, choosing to tackle the easiest part of what she just said first.

"She is," Casey shakes her head as if trying to clear it. "She's just being weird today."

"What kind of cookies is she referring to?"

Casey groans and closes her eyes, her lips moving silently as if she's saying a prayer— probably the serenity prayer. Finally, she tells me "She used to call her virginity her "cookie" as a code word. Kind of like how Monica called hers her 'flower'?"

I look blankly at Casey. I don't know what the hell she's talking about. "Who is Monica?"

She groans again, "From *Friends*!"

Right, because that clears everything right up. Clear as mud. I blink once and continue to stare at her blankly.

"Whatever," she says, shaking her head, clearly exasperated by my presence. "I know you well enough to know you're not going anywhere. And I'm tired of arguing about it. At least I am today."

I look at her and take her in, *really* take her in for the first time today, and I see she looks exhausted. Kind of like how she looked when she arrived home that day. I know better than to point out when a woman looks rough, so I take a different approach.

"You must be tired from your trip. Why didn't you just fly? I only had to leave this morning and I got here before you." She leans back in her chair, crossing her arms over her chest. She's taking a defensive stance. Interesting.

"I don't like to fly," she says simply, shrugging her shoulders and raising her eyebrow as if waiting for me to challenge her. I want to fight with her about as much as she wants to fight with me right now, so I let it go.

"It's not for everyone."

Her eyes widen at my response, or lack thereof. "No, it's not."

I look at the clock on the microwave, eight p.m. I haven't eaten since I grabbed a slice of pizza at the airport on the way to the cab line. I'm starving and right on cue my stomach growls.

"I was about to order some take-out, want something?" she asks, surprising the hell out of me. My eyes dart from the clock to her face, but her vacant expression doesn't let me know what she's thinking.

"That would be great, thanks," I carefully agree, not knowing when the volcano is going to erupt again. "I didn't rent a car, and I'm not sure a cabbie would appreciate taking me to get something to eat *and* finding me a room for the night."

She looks thoughtful for a moment, then stands and grabs a folder from some big organizing thing hanging on a door off to the side of the kitchen—a laundry room maybe? She sets a menu from a health food restaurant in front of me. When I'd been playing baseball, throughout high school and until my shoulder got screwed up in college, I was a clean eater. I wonder if she's throwing this out there because of that, but I know better than to question it when she seems to be extending an olive branch. I don't want her to think I don't appreciate her kindness.

I tell her my order—a turkey and avocado wrap with fresh veggies—and she calls it in. I smile when I hear her order the same thing, only hold the onions. We always had the same food tastes. Whenever we'd go out to eat together, we'd always end up swapping plates halfway through the meal. It was our thing. We had a lot of "things" back then, and I can't help but wonder if we will get the chance to make new "things."

Our late dinner is excellent, the side of mixed fruit surprisingly hit the spot. I catch Casey eyeing me head to toe as I lean back in my chair and stretch my legs out with my arms over my head. It tugs at something inside me, something I thought might have been dormant between us. Not to mention it gives me hope that she's thawing out. Or maybe she's just too exhausted to fight.

"Do you have the number for a cab company?" I ask, breaking her trance.

She startles, blushes from having been caught staring, and looks over at the clock on the microwave. "Decker, it's almost ten o'clock. You can stay in our guest room tonight."

"I don't want to impose-" She clenches her jaw and gives me one of those looks, and I shut my mouth right up. You know the look...it screams, "are you serious right now?"

"If you didn't want to impose, you wouldn't have followed me across the country, now would you?" she says calmly with her hands flat on the table in front of her.

"Right," I nod. "I appreciate this, Case."

"It's fine," she says, getting up from the table. "It's just for tonight. You're going home tomorrow." She fixes me with another glare before picking up her plate and taking it to the sink.

So much for letting that one go. But I'm not going to argue with her. I know deep down she knows damn well I'm not leaving, no matter what she says. I get up and help her clean up the kitchen. Kate had already eaten dinner before she came home earlier, so she didn't join us and has remained in her room the past couple hours.

Casey warns me that the guest room is in between her room and Kate's so I have to be quiet. What the hell did she think I was going to do once I went to bed? Blast my music? Do sit ups and grunt? I dutifully nod and follow her down the hall. She points out the bathroom I'll share with Kate, Casey has a private bath off her bedroom and clearly doesn't want me near her bedroom. Then she points to a door on the right—beside the bathroom—which she says is Kate's room. The room across the hall from Kate's is hers, and the room at the end of the hall, in between the two, is the guest room.

The guest room is really nice. It's painted a light green. There is a dark, cherry wood, queen-sized sleigh bed in the middle of the room, flanked by a couple matching nightstands. A dresser sits off to the side by the window, and a closet with a pocket door is on the other wall.

"My parents would stay in here when they visited. It's why we got a three bedroom," she says absently.

I stop my perusal of the room and look at her just in time to see her eyes well up with tears. I set my duffel down on the bed and step over to her, pulling her into my arms. She folds into me willingly, and I can't say it doesn't make me feel good she came to me so willingly. I half-expected her to swat me away.

Hope.

"Will it ever get easier?" she asks, referring to the loss of her dad, I'm sure.

"I don't know, sweetheart," I say, resting my cheek on top of her head. "But I'll be here for you every day until it does."

She exhales a big breath. I'm not quite sure if it's out of frustration or if she's relieved to have me here, because, in the very next moment, she wraps her arms around me and gives a light squeeze.

Chapter Seventeen

Casey

When I wake in the morning and the events of the previous night unfold in my mind, I can't believe I allowed Decker to spend the night. Even though he was only in the guest room, it was still a moment of weakness I can't afford to have. But what was I supposed to do? Leave him to take a cab and end up at some roach motel because he couldn't do proper research and find a decent place to stay?

No matter what happens between us—or happened between us—I can't do that to Decker. It doesn't make a difference how angry I am with him or how much I try to push him away, he'll always be that six-year-old little boy with the bright green eyes and crazy red hair who'd helped me when I skinned my knee.

I'm sitting at the kitchen table with a big mug of decaf steaming in front of me, rubbing my head with both hands. How did things get so screwed up? I mean, I know how they got screwed up three years ago, but presently? I'm not so sure. I had known there was a chance I'd see Decker when I went back home, I thought I was prepared for that—and maybe I was—but for him to have followed me to California? There is no way I could have prepared myself for that turn of events,

All I know is that I have to get him the hell out of here as soon as possible. Like real soon, too, since I have to leave by 11:45 if I expect to make it to my twelve o'clock appointment on time, and it's already 11:00. Kate left early to take one of her finals, and I feel a smidgen of guilt for proceeding with the take-home tests since I'm back, but I'll worry about that later since I don't have a class scheduled today anyway.

I give myself a quick pep talk—chock full of "be strong" and "you can do it"—and stand from my seat to go wake Decker. I spin around from the table and jump a good foot in the air.

"Damn it, Decker! Can't you wear a bell or something?" I yell, holding my hand to my chest in the hope of slowing down my racing heart.

"Do you always talk to yourself?" he asks, casually stepping around me and walking over to the coffee pot. I must give him a confused look, because he proceeds to explain. "Yesterday, you were talking to your purse, or your keys, I'm not really sure which." He shakes his head at the apparent oddity that is me. Whatever. "Then just now it sounds like you were trying to amp yourself up for something."

"First of all, if I was talking to my purse or my keys then I would be talking to an inanimate object, not to myself." I watch as he takes a mug off the rack hanging on the wall and pours himself a cup of coffee like he lives here. It both irks me and makes me feel warm inside. I kind of like having him in my California home.

Stop that line of thinking right now, Casey!

"Admitting to talking to inanimate objects doesn't really help your case, you know?"

I growl—yes growl—at him as he sits down at the table and picks up the newspaper Kate must have grabbed from the doorstep this morning. "Make yourself at home, Decker!" I shout, rather immaturely, before stomping off to my room. I swear I hear him chuckle from behind me. I've never wanted to hit him so bad in my life. Ugh. One minute he makes me feel warm and tingly all over and the next he just chaps my ass with his arrogance.

I go into my bathroom and proceed with my morning routine. Ignoring, for now, the

Decker-sized elephant in my kitchen. He's not going to go away easily. Not that I didn't assume this before, but he's making it clear now.

I undress and slip into the shower, doing a light scrub of my hair and body since I had a thorough cleaning when I got home yesterday and haven't done much since except sleep and eat. My shampoo is citrus scented and my body wash is apple, so it's quite the pick-me-up and just what I need. By the time I'm done, I feel rejuvenated.

I dry myself off and dress in a simple outfit of skinny jeans and a dark pink tank top. I slip on my flip flops and head back out to the kitchen. I don't bother with makeup—not anymore—but I do grab my lip gloss out of my purse that's resting on the small table in the entryway. Applying it to my lips, I look towards the kitchen.

"You need to go," I tell him. "I've got places to be." I cross my arms over my chest and cock my hip to the side, tapping my foot like I mean business.

Decker laughs at my display. "Whatever you say, sunshine." He gets up from the table and puts his now empty coffee mug in the dishwasher. "Will you drop me off somewhere?"

"The airport?" I ask, hopefully.

He sighs and looks disappointed. "No, not the airport. A hotel. Preferably an extended stay." He pointedly looks at me, daring me to argue. Just as I suspected, he's not going anywhere, and he wants me to know it.

"Fine. But hurry up or I'm going to be late." I stomp over to the couch and sit down, picking up a magazine to leaf through while I wait for him to get dressed. Out of the corner of my eye I watch him stand there for a moment, then leave the kitchen. I know he feels dejected by the blatant fact that I don't want him here, but I can't let myself care about that. I can't look into his eyes—those same eyes that were so sad when I tried to send him away fifteen years ago—they'll break me down.

He emerges from the hallway a few minutes later, his duffel bag hanging over his shoulder by the long strap. He's just so handsome, even in a plain white t-shirt and holey jeans. He'll make a girl very happy one day. It just won't be me. It can never be me.

"Let's go," I say. I rise from the couch and grab my bag off the table. "There's an extended stay right down the street."

He silently follows me out the door and down the steps. As we approach the car and I unlock the door, he finally speaks. "Thanks, Casey."

I look at him over the roof of the car, the sunlight providing the perfect backdrop for this beautiful man. Decker. My best friend. "You're welcome." I'd smile, but I can't. If I did, the tears I'm trying so desperately to hold in would come out.

***

"Everything looks good, Casey," Dr. Smythe says as he finishes his exam. "You're blood pressure is a little high, though."

"Isn't that to be expected? I mean considering what's been going on?"

"Yes, it's not uncommon for blood pressure to rise in stressful situations. But I'd like to run a few tests just in case." He jots some notes down on his tablet. "I'll send Rebecca in to draw blood."

"Okay." He exits the room and I sit on the exam table, kicking my legs back and forth in front of me like a child would.

After a few minutes alone with only my thoughts, I realize I can't stop thinking about Decker. I'd dropped him off at the extended stay before heading to my appointment. I'd felt like a complete asshole—still do—for leaving him there. It had seemed like a nice enough place, frequented by out-of-town business folk and visitors to the university, but it wasn't a home. How could I just leave my best friend there when I clearly had room for him at my place?

I shake the thoughts out of my head. He can't stay at my place, I remind myself. He needs to go back home. He can't stay here forever anyway, he has a year left at the

University of South Carolina and he needs to finish his studies. He needs to think about his future. His future that doesn't—can't—include me.

My thoughts are interrupted as Rebecca—Becky, as I like to call her—enters the room with her little vampire cart. She's about four years older than I am, with black hair cut into a severe bob and dark brown eyes. She's absolutely gorgeous and of Asian descent, though I'm not sure of the exact ethnicity as I've never been bold enough to ask about her heritage. She's a phlebotomist—and a damn good one at that—I can never feel her sticks.

"We've got five to fill today," she says, waving the little vials in front of my face.

"Yay," I say with absolutely no enthusiasm.

She smirks at me. "Lean back," she says, and I listen. She ties off my arm with the pinchy rubber band, gives me a stress ball to squeeze, and proceeds to do her thing. I'm feeling kind of sleepy, still exhausted from my trip, so I close my eyes.

Chapter Eighteen

Decker

It's been about four hours since Casey dropped me off and I'm currently laying on the firm hotel bed wondering what she's doing. If you'd asked me on the flight here what I thought I'd be doing on my second day in California, this is definitely not what I would have said. Not that I'd expected Casey to welcome me with open arms or anything, not with the way we left things back home, but I guess part of me had hoped she'd at least offer me her couch. I know, not the brightest tool in the box, or however that saying goes.

Earlier, I'd had lunch at a little café about a block away from the hotel. Their chicken salad was good, but not as good as my momma makes it. California is so different from home. Yeah, I've only been to this one part and most of my time has been spent inside Casey's apartment and the hotel, but I've seen enough to know it's not the same. Charleston is smaller, older. Casey always loved the quaintness of our Holy City; I'm not sure how she makes it out here. Especially on her own. I'm already home sick, and I've only been here one day.

I roll over to my side and grab my cell phone from the nightstand. I look through my notifications and social media. Aside from a few hilarious cat videos, nothing excites me. I briefly entertain the thought of booking my return flight, but immediately shake that thought out of my head. I'm not giving up. Something tells me Casey needs me. She needs me to not give up on her, whether she realizes it or not.

Tapping around my phone, I find her name in my contacts. I snuck a picture of her when she was home last week and assigned that to her profile. It's of one of her more peaceful moments, taken while she was sleeping. The early morning light coming in through the sheer white curtains of her bedroom gave her soft skin a beautiful glow. She'd looked like an angel—my angel—and I hadn't been able to resist capturing the moment.

Should I call her? Text her? She probably would have reached out to me if she wanted to talk...

I sigh and roll onto my back. Is this what women go through when they exchange numbers with a guy? Because I'm starting to feel like a total douche for tossing girls' numbers all three years at college.

Screw it.

Me: Hey.

Yeah, that was smooth. Took me five minutes to decide if I wanted to text "hey."

I wait for her response. Five minutes. Ten minutes. Thirty minutes.

"What the hell am I doing?" I ask myself. Great, now I'm the one talking to myself.

I roll over and get off the bed. After slipping on my sneakers, I make sure I've got my wallet and my key card and head out of the room. I'm on the ground floor, which is both good and bad. Good because it's easy to get in and out. Bad because I get all the street noise.

The drive over here with Casey earlier was short, so I think that by using the map on my iPhone, I'll be able to navigate back to her place on foot. If she's not going to answer me, I'm going to go to her. Simple as that. I'm nothing if not persistent.

As I walk, for the first time since my flight landed, I am thankful I'm in California. The less than ten minute drive turned out to be an hour walk. If I'd done that in South Carolina, I'd have gotten heat stroke—and I'm an athlete, or was one anyway. It was ninety degrees when I'd left yesterday. But here in Cali, I'm barely breaking a sweat.

The two long flights of stairs going up to the third floor are still a bear, though. I don't think it matters what kind of shape you're in. How these girls do this daily, I can't tell you. I'd have moved to a ground floor unit. There are very few stairs in my life back home and the steps in the lecture halls are nothing like this concrete hell.

I make it to their apartment door and knock, embarrassed at my loss of breath. I need to get back into cardio. I'd seen Casey's car in the lot when I got here, so I know she's home. I hear movement on the other side of the door, and after a moment, a wide-eyed Kate answers the door.

"Hey, Decker. What are you doing here?" she asks, pleasantly enough even though she has the door opened only wide enough to fit her head through.

"I came to see Casey, is she busy?"

"Um, no. She's not busy," Kate answers reluctantly, still not opening the door any wider.

"Can I see her?" I ask.

Kate lets out a small sigh. "She's resting."

"Resting? Is she not feeling well?" I step a little closer, ready to go to Casey's aid.

Kate looks over her shoulder quickly, then quietly slips out the door so she's standing in the breezeway with me. "She'll be mad that I told you this," she starts, and I don't speak because I get the impression she'll stop talking to me if I do. "But she fainted at the doctor's office today."

"She *what*?" I raise my voice, causing Kate to take a step back. "I'm sorry. I'm sorry," I say at a normal volume. "Is she okay?"

Kate looks like she wants to say more, but instead simply nods. "She was having some routine bloodwork. Said it's probably just due to exhaustion and poor diet."

I shake my head, I knew she didn't look well when she showed up here yesterday. Hell, she didn't look well when she was home either. "Can I see her?" I ask Kate, with my best puppy dog begging eyes.

She rolls her eyes at the obvious ruse to get what I want. "Come on in," she says, opening the door quietly and holding her index finger up to her mouth, letting me know to be quiet. "She's probably still asleep," she whispers. "Just go on back, but don't piss her off."

I give her a look, "Right. Have you met her? Apparently my breathing pisses her off lately."

Kate looks at me thoughtfully, "I don't know, Decker. You may be just what we need." Then she turns around and walks off into the kitchen. I have *no* idea how to take what she just said, so I shake it off and walk down the hall to Casey's room.

I saw the door last night and this morning, but I hadn't actually seen inside her room. She didn't invite me in, and, hell, she'll probably get pissed that I'm coming in now, but she'll just have to get over it. I don't like that she's not well, and I want to see her with my own two eyes. The door is open a crack, so I slowly push it the rest of the way, praying the hinge doesn't squeak—it doesn't.

The first thing I see when I open the door is my girl. She's resting on her side, curled up in a ball on her bed, facing the wall. Her bed surprises me. It's so...fluffy. Her blankets and pillows are all white, and the pillows are everywhere. They're all along the light-colored wooden headboard and around Casey. Some have even spilled off onto the floor. Casey was always into simple things growing up, so to see her lying on this...this cloud...is just weird. But damn, at least she looks comfortable.

I take a moment to take in the rest of the room before she wakes and kicks me out. The walls are a light blue which really emphasizes her cloud bed. There isn't anything hanging on the walls, but she does have a photo collage frame on her nightstand. I carefully pick it up, since I'm now standing way too close to her sleeping form. The collage makes me smile; it holds photos of her with her parents, her with Kate, and her with me.

Almost three thousand miles and three years between us and I'm one of the four people on her nightstand. Things suddenly don't feel so hopeless after all.

Chapter Nineteen

Casey

I wake to a dark bedroom, and the events of the day flash through my mind. Decker in my apartment this morning. Dropping Decker off at the hotel. The doctor's visit. I'd passed out as Becky sucked five vials of blood from my body. How embarrassing. Dr. Smythe had said it was most likely due to my being run-down. Or rather "not taking care of myself," as he'd put it.

My bedroom is pitch black. I must have slept all afternoon since night has fallen. I suddenly realize I'm very warm—no, hot—and there is some kind of pressure on my chest. I have a moment of dread, worrying if I really did run myself down too far this time. My chest tightens as the anxiety begins to overtake me. Then I look down and see the arm that's wrapped tightly around me. A male arm.

What the hell?

I slowly turn my head to look over my shoulder and at first I'm struck by relief that I'm not getting sick, then I feel annoyance because what the heck is he doing here? In my bed? Wrapped around me like a glove. Hadn't I thrown him out this morning?

Dammit, Decker! Always inserting yourself where you don't belong.

Dammit, Kate, too! Somebody had to have let him in, and it clearly wasn't me.

Very slowly and carefully, I roll over and try to extricate myself from his hold without waking him. No such luck. In mid-roll, his grip tightens, and he sighs in contentment. *I wish I could feel so at peace.* I huff and resign myself to being stuck in the prison of his arms. Can't say it's all that terrible.

"Don't sound so miserable. You might give a guy a complex," he rasps out in that sexy, husky, sleepy man voice.

My body betrays my mind as I tingle all over. Then, snapping out of my trance, I elbow him in the ribs and sit up as he grunts.

"That was harsh, Case," he chuckles, rubbing his ribs. I make the mistake of looking down at him. He's shirtless, *the sonofabitch*, looking so much more like a man than the boy I left behind years ago. His abs are ripped—which shouldn't surprise me because he was in excellent shape back in high school, just not as defined. I guess I'd assumed he hadn't kept it up since he couldn't play ball anymore. I assumed wrong.

"My eyes are up here," he says, and I scan my way up, from his abs to his face, where he wears a shit-eating grin.

I roll my eyes. "Whatever. You're such an ass." I scoot down to the end of the bed and stand up. I'm immediately lightheaded so I close my eyes, reaching out in front of me to brace myself on my dresser.

Decker's behind me in an instant. "Are you okay?" he asks, placing his hands on the sides of my ribs in an effort to help keep me upright.

I nod my head slowly. "A little dizzy, I guess." I don't say any more than that since I don't know how much Kate told him.

He gently turns me around to face him. "Kate mentioned you passed out getting some blood drawn," he says, his brows furrowed and concern etching his features. "Is everything, okay? Why were you having blood drawn?"

"It was just a routine checkup," I lie, side-stepping out of his grasp. "I was pretty run down from my trip, my blood pressure was off, the doctor just wanted to run some tests."

"Makes sense, I guess, given what happened with your dad," he says, nodding in understanding.

I tilt my head at him in question, unsure of what he's talking about—wait, does he know? He can't possibly! And then it hits me. "Yeah, family medical history and all."

I frown, thinking about my dad. Why is it that it's not until people die that we realize all the things we should have done while they were alive? I wish I'd gone to more baseball and hockey games with him. I wish I'd said yes every time he asked me to go fishing. I wish I'd spent more times on the couch with him on Sundays watching the races. Instead, I snubbed him over and over again for homework. A lot of good graduating at the top of my class is doing me now...but those extra moments with my dad? Those would have stayed with me forever, especially now that he's gone.

"I'm sorry," Decker says, breaking me out of my reverie. He walks over and gives me a hug. "I miss him, too."

The familiarity of being in his arms, his soothing voice, and the fact that he truly gets me is what breaks me down. I choke on a sob.

"Shh, it's okay. Let it out, sweetheart."

And I do. I curl my fists against his bare chest and sob. "I m-miss him s-so m-much."

"I know, baby. I know." He rubs my back and holds me tight. "It's going to be okay, Casey. I know it might not seem like it now. But it'll get better."

I want to scream at him, ask him how the hell he knows it will get better, but I don't. I let him hold me and whisper words of encouragement in my ear. I let him lay me down on my bed and cuddle me, holding me so close to his body it seems that he's the one seeking comfort, not me.

And maybe that is what he's doing. My dad *was* like a second dad to him. Has he taken a moment to grieve his loss? While I'd been at home, he spent most of that time focused on me. Making sure I'd been okay...that I was eating and sleeping.

Once the floodgates finally dry up, I look up to him and find him staring right back at me. I could get lost in those comforting green orbs. "I'm sorry, Decker."

"Wh-" he starts, but I hold my hand up to stop him.

"No, let me finish," I plead. He nods, and I continue. "I'm sorry for your loss, too. You and my dad were close. I know you used to go off and do guy stuff with him and your dad. Even after I left." He looks at me with questions in his eyes. "My parents told me when we talked," I shrugged. "I'm sorry I've been such a basket case, and you had to spend so much time taking care of me back home. And I'm sorry that no one was taking care of you."

He sighs. "Casey, I was doing exactly what I was supposed to be doing all that time. Being there for you. It's what I wanted to do, and it's what your dad would have wanted me to do. You may not have seen me grieve, but I did. In my own way, I did."

I rest my head against his firm chest and nod.

"He went with my dad to a lot of my home games, you know?" I nod again but don't speak, hoping he takes this opportunity to get things off his chest...to grieve. "Even after you were gone, he'd still ask me to go fishing when I was home, or hunting if the season was right. Sometimes my dad would join us...sometimes he wouldn't. I felt closer to you when I was with your dad. I know that probably sounds weird, but it's true. He never betrayed your confidence, even when I pressed him. He never said anything other than 'she's doing okay,' or 'she's good.' I both loved and hated him for that. I appreciated any little bit he'd share, but I also wanted more. I kind of think he liked spending time with me for the same reason I liked spending time with him. It made us both feel closer to you, even if we didn't talk about you."

My eyes are filled with tears again as I listen to him speak. I'm finally getting a small sense of what Decker went through when I left, of what my dad went through. He'd always told me he understood my decision to stay in California. But jeez, what else was he going to say to me while I'd been going through my own personal hell? Of course they'd agree with anything I threw out there. I'd thought my actions had been selfless. Turns out they'd been rather selfish.

I can't go back in time to fix things with my dad, but I still have time to fix things with my mom, and maybe even with Decker. There's got to be a way to make peace with them without letting the walls I've built around myself come crumbling down.

Chapter Twenty

Casey

For the second time in less than twenty-four hours, I wake up in Decker's arms. But instead of trying to sneak away, I revel in his warmth. Decker. My best friend. Today is the day I start trying to make things right. Life is too short to have regrets. I regret not spending more time with my dad before he died. I need to make sure I make up for lost time with my mom...and with Decker.

No regrets.

I nestle deeper into Decker's familiar, comforting embrace and let out a sigh of contentment. That same sigh Decker made last night that I'd been both envious of and irritated by. I smile at the thought and feel him begin to stir.

"To what do I owe the pleasure? Oh wait, you're not fully awake, are you? If you're going to flip on me, at least give me a warning so I can get out of your reach before you strike." He starts slowly moving his body away from me.

I giggle into his chest, his light smattering of chest hair tickling my nose. "Good morning, Decker."

Realizing I'm not going to go ape-shit on him, at least not yet, he relaxes back into position, pulling me back against him with his free arm. "Good morning, Case." I can hear the smile in his voice.

I clear my throat, making Decker aware that what I'm about to say is pretty important. "I'd like for you to stay at the apartment while you're here, not at the hotel. I'm going to talk to Kate today, but I don't think she'll have a problem with it."

Decker pulls his head back and looks down at me. "Are you sure you're okay with that?"

I sigh, knowing that my actions over the past couple weeks, hell, over the past three years up to and including yesterday, have caused him to question my newfound effort. "Yes, I'm sure. I want to start fresh with us. Or continue fresh, or whatever," I shake my head, knowing I sound stupid but unable to do anything about it. I am stupid for keeping him out of my life this long. "Life's too short, Decker. I want you in mine."

"Not that I'm complaining or anything," he begins, "but you do realize that's a contradictory statement, right?" I look up at him, and he laughs at the strange expression on my face.

"I was the valedictorian, Decker," I state in an obnoxiously pompous manner.

He laughs and pats my head like he's pacifying a child. "I know. I'm just saying...life is the longest thing anyone ever does. It's kinda funny how we think it's short."

Decker may be right, but it doesn't make me feel any differently about it.

***

After we get out of bed, I call Kate at work and ask her about letting Decker stay with us. She surprises me by immediately agreeing and even adding that he can stay as long as he wants. Not sure why she's so uncharacteristically enthusiastic about it, but I don't have time to wonder because I need to take Decker back to the extended stay to get his things before the eleven a.m. check-out. I feel like a jerk for making him go yesterday when he hadn't even ended up sleeping there.

We have lunch at a small sandwich shop near campus and Decker tells me about some new restaurants back home he thinks I'll love. We automatically swap the other halves of our sandwiches halfway through our meal, and I smile at how easy it is to fall into familiar routines with Decker. But I must remind myself...we can't fall into *all* our old routines. Not this time. This time we're friends...just friends.

He asks me to show him Stanford, so when we leave the restaurant I head in that direction. I drive through campus slowly, pointing out the buildings where I've had various classes, the cafeteria, library, and finally ending up at the baseball field.

"Did you ever miss it?" he asks as I pull into a parking space near the Sunken Diamond, the aptly named, recessed baseball field.

"Miss what?"

"Home. Charleston. This place is so different." He's not looking at me, but out the window at the surrounding scenery.

"Of course I missed Charleston. There's no place like home." And I did miss it. The place and the people.

"You didn't come back. Not once." He doesn't say it in an accusatory way. He's just pointing out the obvious.

I know I need to respond in some way, but what can I say? What can I tell him without telling him everything? Because I can't tell him that. Not today and maybe not ever.

"I just had a lot going on here, Decker." There, that's not a lie. Just a half-truth.

"Plenty of college students have a lot going on and still return home for the summer. For Thanksgiving. For Christmas. What was so important that it kept you away?"

I sigh. "Decker..."

"Just forget it. If you're going to feed me another line," he snaps, "I don't want to hear it."

"Decker, I'm—"

"Can we just go? I'm tired. I didn't get much sleep last night."

I don't know if that was a barb at me or not, but it hurts just the same. I turn on the car and pull out of the parking space. "I'm sorry," I say. I whisper it so quietly that I'm sure he didn't hear me, but the fact that he reaches his left hand over the console and grabs my right hand tells me he did. And I feel a smidge better.

We ride in silence back to the apartment, my hand in his, and both of our heads full of who knows what. When we get back, he excuses himself to the guest room, and I drop down onto the couch, mentally spent. I don't know how I'm going to let Decker back in while still keeping him at arm's length. But I can't tell him what happened freshman year. I can't tell him what's still going on as a result of it. It would break him.

I hear the front door unlock and look up to see Kate slip in, as graceful as ever, even though she's carrying about twelve grocery bags. I jump up to help her.

"What is all this?" I laugh as I take all the bags from her right hand. I think we are the reason that Internet meme exists about carrying fifty bags in from the car rather than making two trips.

"You said Decker was staying. We need more food since someone was too busy passing out yesterday to go to the grocery store," she smirks at me. I'm glad she's able to make light of the situation now, because when I called her from the doctor's office yesterday she was in full-blown panic mode.

"Thanks, Kate. I should have gone while Decker and I were out today but things got kinda heavy, and I didn't even think about it."

"Heavy in a good way? Or heavy in a bad way?" she winks.

My. Roommate. Winks.

Since when?

"What is *up* with you?" I ask.

Her eyes quickly dart from the grocery bags to me and back to the bags. "What do you mean?"

"You're acting so weird. Different. Since I've been back. What's going on?"

"Nothing," she answers way too quickly. So of course I don't believe her.

"Kate," I say firmly.

"Casey," she matches my tone.

"Whatever."

"Tell me about you and Decker," she says, changing the subject and continuing with her task of putting the groceries away. I make a face at all the vegetables she's putting in the fridge's crisper drawer.

"There's nothing to tell."

"Right. That's why you went from sending him away to letting him stay here?" She looks at me knowingly, raising her eyebrow.

I lean back against the counter and cross my arms over my chest. "I decided to give the whole friend thing a chance." She smiles wide in response. "Don't get too excited, I'm still not sure I'm gonna tell him anything."

She frowns. "Why the heck not?"

I shake my head. "I just don't know if I can, okay? Let me do this my way. I want the chance to make new memories with Decker. I don't want to regret the lost time like I do...like I do with my dad."

"Oh sweetie," she says, frowning as she steps over to me and pulls me into a hug. "You know there's a way for you to ensure lots of chances for memories."

I pull out of her embrace. "No. Just no."

She grimaces. "Sorry, Casey. But I still think you're being dumb. I respect your wishes because ultimately it's your decision. But you're an idiot." She turns away from me and puts away the last of the groceries, slamming the refrigerator, cabinet, and pantry doors.

I scowl at her back while she proceeds to ignore me, then finally stomp off to my room. Whatever. I've made my decision, and I don't care what anyone else thinks.

Chapter Twenty-One

Decker

I can't help but overhear Casey and Kate's conversation in the kitchen. Yeah, maybe I was eavesdropping. I have no shame, not when it comes to helping Casey. And now I know with complete certainty that Casey is hiding something from me. Her vague conversation with Kate proves it, and I *will* find out what it is.

The words Kate had spoken to me yesterday before letting me into Casey's room come back into my mind.

"I don't know, Decker. You may be just what we need."

What had she meant by that?

Only one way to find out. I know Casey's in her room because I just heard the door slam shut after she presumably stormed off. And I know Kate is still in the kitchen because I can still hear her slamming shit.

Women.

I carefully open the bedroom door and silently sneak past Casey's room as I creep towards the kitchen. "Hey," I say as I enter, causing Kate to jump.

"You scared the hell out of me!" she says, clutching her hand to her chest. "We're going to need to get you a bell." I laugh because Casey said the same thing yesterday. Maybe I should quit the sports medicine route and look into a career as a ninja.

"Sorry," I say, shrugging my shoulders. "It's not like you would have been able to hear me approach over all that racket." I gesture to the cabinet doors she had been slamming.

She blushes when she realizes I'd caught her little performance. "Sorry about that," she says. "Casey just gets me so riled up sometimes."

That's right, talk about Casey.

"What were you two arguing about?"

"You heard that?" she asks, her eyes wide.

I nod. "Kind of hard not to."

She looks down at the linoleum. "It's nothing."

"You seem a little too pissed off for it to be nothing."

She blows a breath out. "Look, Casey's just got some issues that I've been trying to get her to open up about it but she won't. She's the most stubborn person I know."

"Don't I know it." I laugh and she joins in.

"Right, you would know." She shakes her head again. "I like you, Decker, but I can't betray her trust. I'm sorry."

I sigh. Figures. Kate's a smart girl; she'd probably known from the moment I'd opened my mouth what I was after. "I understand. I just want to help in any way that I can. If you have any suggestions on how I can do that, please tell me."

She gives me a genuine smile and, if I'm not mistaken, looks a bit relieved...as though a small weight has been lifted. "I definitely will."

"Listen, what you said last night," I say, "about me being just what you guys need?"

She looks down again. "I shouldn't have said anything."

I nod. "Right."

"Casey has missed you. A lot. That's all." She gives me a half smile and returns to her groceries, though much quieter now.

I know that's not what she'd meant when she'd said it yesterday. At least it's not the whole truth. Maybe one day I'll get enough partial truths to form the whole truth. Maybe.

***

Casey finally emerges from her bedroom as I'm sitting on the couch, flipping between real estate and home renovation shows.

"I'm sorry about earlier, Decker," she says, sitting next to me on the couch and curling up into my side.

"It's alright, Case," I tell her, even though it's really not okay at all. I lower my arm from the back of the couch to wrap around her shoulder.

"I have to go back to work tomorrow," she says.

"Where do you work?" How do I not know something as simple as that?

"I work as an admin at a small mental health clinic. It's just part-time so I can get some extra cash and pad my resume a bit in my field."

"Do you like it?"

She looks to be considering her response. That's the Casey I remember...thinking before

~ 170 ~

she speaks. "I don't like doing administrative work. I am not a fan of filing, copying, and all that clerical stuff. But I like the place. The staff are really nice, and they know my major is psych so they talk to me about stuff. Not actual patient stuff though because that's confidential, but they tell me about the job. The things they like and dislike. They answer my questions and sometimes help me on subjects I'm struggling with."

"That sounds nice." Though I can't imagine Casey struggling with anything.

"It is," she smiles and I can tell that despite her few cons, she really is happy there. "Do you work back home?"

"No," I say, feeling ashamed. "I didn't have time while I was playing, and since I've been injured...I haven't really had the motivation, I guess."

"Were you—are you—depressed?" she asks carefully.

I look down into her big brown eyes, wide with concern, and for the first time since I've ever known Casey, I want to lie to her. I don't want her to know the truth. I don't want her to know that I had battled depression in the months that followed the injury. And I really don't want her to know that as bad as I'd felt when my career was over, it hadn't been nearly as bad as the things I'd felt when she left me—back then I'd felt like my entire life was over.

But I can't lie to her. "Yes, I was depressed."

She frowns. "I'm so sorry I wasn't there for you, Decker. I wish my parents had told me. I honestly don't know if it would have made a difference, but I'd like to think that it would have. That I would have at least called you." She nuzzles her head into my side and I feel my shirt dampen from her silent tears.

"Hey," I say, lifting her chin with my finger so she's looking in my eyes. "No tears. We both made mistakes. We're here together now. We're fixing things. We can't go back. Only forward. And we're going to go forward together." I hold her gaze and see what may be hesitation in her eyes, but before I can say anything about it, it's gone.

She gives me a small smile and nods. "I'd like that."

"Me too," I say, relieved she'd actually agreed with me.

We settle in more comfortably on the couch. Me leaning on the arm with my right elbow up. Her leaning against me with her legs tucked to the side. It's familiar...it's home. Then she says the most wonderful words.

"I'm going to go home for the summer."

I can't stop the smile from spreading across my face. "Really?"

She can hear the elation in my voice and laughs as she pats my stomach. "Yes, really. I'm going to tell my boss today. I'll have to work out the two weeks, or until they can find a replacement, but it shouldn't be too hard with school letting out. Lots of students are going to be looking for summer jobs."

This is the best news I've had in a long time. I thought I'd be here most of the summer begging her to come home, but that's not the case. She's decided to do it all on her own.

"Have you told your mom yet?"

"No." She shakes her head. "I was planning on calling her tonight."

"She's gonna be really happy."

She sighs. "I know."

"What's wrong?" I look down, but her face is hidden behind her long hair.

"Nothing. But it's only for the summer, Decker. I'll come back here in August. I just don't want you to get too excited because I'm just going to be gone again. Just don't get too used to having me around. My mom needs to realize that, too."

I tighten my arm that's around her shoulder and pull her closer to me. "You'll be home for two months, Case. That's two more months than I've seen you in years. I'm gonna be excited, so is your mom and my parents, and you're gonna deal with it."

She laughs lightly, but still seems tense. "I guess so."

I write it off as her being nervous about being back home after so long, especially since she'll be returning to a home without her dad. Her sadness upsets me, but I can't help but feel excited that this summer will give us two months to get to know each other again.

This summer might end up being the best summer of my life. Well, second best. The best was that summer fifteen years ago when I stumbled upon that little girl with the brown hair and brown eyes. The prettiest girl I'd ever seen.

Chapter Twenty-Two

Casey

To say my mother had been excited when I called is an understatement. When I'd told her I was coming home for the summer, she shrieked in my ear for a good five minutes before Decker finally took the phone away and promised her he'd get me home safely.

Twenty-seven hundred miles in the car with Decker Abrams. That's going to be interesting. It'll be nice to share the drive, but there will be so many hours in close quarters with him. I have no idea how I'm going to keep my cool, in more ways than one, but I've got two weeks to figure it out.

On my way to work, I dropped Decker off at the campus library so he could work on his finals. I didn't feel comfortable leaving him at the apartment for eight hours. It's not that I don't trust him—I do—I'm just afraid he might find something I don't want him to find. He'd actually suggested the library, so it was perfect. Now I'll just need to figure out what to do with him for my other five shifts over the next two weeks.

I arrive at the clinic fifteen minutes early so I can meet with Sharon, my supervisor, and give my notice for the summer. I've worked here for almost two years now, and, with the exception of my dad's death, I've never requested a day off, let alone two months.

I quietly knock on Sharon's open door. She looks up from a mess of paperwork and smiles at me. "Casey! Come on in!" She gestures to the chair in front of her desk as she neatly stacks her papers and sets them aside. After I'm seated, she turns on her concern. "You doing okay?"

I nod at her. This is my first time back at work, my first time speaking with her, since taking the time off to go home. "It's still hard to think about...to talk about...but I'm okay."

She smiles sadly. Sharon isn't one of the clinic's staff with the "Ph.D." at the end of her name, and she doesn't need it as the facility's manager, but she is a licensed therapist. She's never tried to shrink me, though I'm sure she wants to. Everyone who knows my story wants to. She's in her mid-thirties, tall and very beautiful, with wavy brown hair and bright blue eyes. But, she's surprisingly single. With her positivity and confidence, I'm certain it's intentional.

"So what's going on?" Even though she hasn't seen me in a couple weeks, she doesn't make small talk, which I appreciate. My dad's passing is still pretty raw, and I'm not quite ready to talk about it, especially with a counselor—paid or not.

I make eye contact and see in her eyes that she knows exactly why I'm here. She's really good at reading people. "I've decided to go home for the summer."

The smile on her knowing face brightens. "That's great."

I give a small smile, agreeing with her as I fidget my hands in my lap. "Is two weeks enough notice? I can stay longer. I don't have to go back right away. And I'll be back. You know, in the fall?"

Sharon raises her hand for me to pause. "Slow down, Casey. It's fine. Two weeks is fine. In fact, tomorrow would be fine. We still have the temp on hand who was working for you while you were out. Plus, Claire just told me yesterday that she'd like more hours for the summer." Claire was the other part-time admin who worked on my off days.

"I would like to work out the two weeks, if that's okay," I tell her, even though I can clearly tell I'm not needed. I know she doesn't mean any harm by it, it's more like she wants me to take an actual break, one that's not for a hospital visit or funeral. And she wants me to do it before I change my mind. As I said, two years without requesting any leave.

She nods, still smiling. "I figured as much. Of course you can work out your two weeks."

"Thank you," I say, standing up.

"You're welcome, Casey. I'm going to miss you around here this summer. It'll be strange not having you around that long, but I'm so glad you're spending some time back home. It'll be good for you."

I nod, hurrying out of her office and down the short hallway to my desk in the file room. My inbox is empty and no paperwork needs to be filed. I lean back in my chair and sigh. I know I'm not indispensable by any means, but it's still a bit depressing knowing you're so easily replaceable.

***

Kate's working tonight, so after work I take Decker to one of mine and Kate's favorite Italian restaurants in San Francisco. As much as I love some good South Carolina cuisine, I'm going to miss the food here this summer. And the wine. And the Ghirardelli chocolate.

"Where'd you go just now?" Decker asks as he sops up the last of his marinara sauce with a piece of Italian bread.

"Just thinking about how I'll miss this food," I tell him with a small smile. "Kind of a silly thing to be thinking about."

"It's not silly. But I'm sure you haven't forgotten about all the food Charleston has to offer."

"No, I haven't forgotten." All I can think about is how rich and delicious it all is, and how I'll have to seriously pace myself.

"What's the first think you want to have when we get back?"

I twirl the pasta on my fork as I consider his question. "Shrimp and grits," I say with a smile. "Your momma's shrimp and grits."

His responding grin is huge. "Now that we can arrange. What else?"

"Lowcountry boil."

"My dad's?" he asks, still grinning.

"That would be amazing, but I can't expect your parents to cook all my meals."

"As if they'd mind. I think they've been waiting for you to come home as much as your parents."

I frown at his words. It's *parent*. I only have one parent now. Singular, not plural. I set down my fork and push my plate away.

Decker sighs, frowning for the first time since I'd said I was going home. "I'm sorry, Casey. I wasn't thinking."

I shrug. "It's okay, Decker. It's only been a couple weeks. It's not something you just get used to."

"But I ruined this," he says, referring to the good time we'd been having.

I give him my best forced smile. "You didn't ruin anything. How about we get out of here and get some gelato?"

"Now you're speaking my language!" His bright smile instantly returns.

I laugh at his enthusiasm as he flags down our waiter and asks for the check. He's always had a sweet tooth—a chocolate sweet tooth. He leaves some cash in the folder and hurries me out of the restaurant. We walk the quick two blocks over to the closest gelato place—well, I try to walk, but since he's holding my hand and practically running, I'm being dragged.

"Let me guess what flavor you want," he says, browsing the labeled tubs inside the glass display. The shop is loud and full of other patrons desperate for a cool treat on this unusually warm night. "I want to say vanilla bean, but I think you're going to go with amaretto."

"And you'd be right," I say, winking at him. *Wait, why did I just wink at him?*

He catches it and smirks. "And I'll get the double chocolate."

"Of course," I say, rolling my eyes.

"What? Don't knock the chocolatey deliciousness." He gives me a pretend offended look, and I laugh. I miss playful Decker.

"I miss playful Casey, too," he says with a small smile. Whoops, I guess I said that last part out loud.

"I'm sorry, Decker," I say, but he shushes me with his finger to my lips. I freeze at the contact, yet still feel warm all over.

"Not tonight. Tonight we have fun." Slightly frozen from his touch, I nod my acceptance. He slowly, almost seductively, removes his finger from my lips, and we order our gelatos.

Decker and I walk the dark streets of San Francisco, eating our gelatos and laughing at stories from when we were kids and when we'd been apart. He tells me more about his injury and the surgeries he went through, what it had been like to stop playing ball. I tell him a bit more about school and my life in San Francisco, careful to leave certain parts out.

~ 181 ~

All in all, it was a great night with my best friend.

Yeah...Decker's still my best friend.

Chapter Twenty-Three

Casey

A couple days after our Italian night in San Francisco, Decker declares he wants to cook me dinner. I'd just gotten home from work, and he practically plowed me over, grabbing my keys and rushing out the door. I stood in the entryway in a stunned silence.

"What the hell just happened?"

Kate starts laughing at me from the kitchen. "He's been like a caged animal all day. Practically bouncing off of every surface in this place. We played two games of Monopoly, Casey. Two! Do you know how much time it takes to play two games of

Monopoly? I was about to ask Dr. Vasquez if he had any ketamine."

Dr. Vasquez is our neighbor across the hall. He's a veterinarian. I highly doubt he has any ketamine on hand in his apartment, but the thought of Decker being tranquilized makes me laugh nonetheless. Growing up he was always pretty hyper, but I never minded. I fed off of it.

"Thanks for hanging out with him today," I tell her, finally shutting the front door and setting my purse and keys down on the side table. She smiles sympathetically. She knows why I didn't want to leave Decker alone in the apartment.

"You know, you could just tell him."

"No, I can't," I say with a sigh.

"What's the big deal?" she asks, and I glare at her. "Seriously, Casey. You can use all the support you can get."

"That's the thing!" I shout, raising my hands and slapping them down on my hips. "I already get babied enough by you and my mom. I don't need anyone else tiptoeing around me. I'm fine."

"You're *not* fine. But whatever. You know I'm not going to say anything. But *you* should. He deserves to know."

"Whatever," I shake my head and storm over to the couch, flopping down with a thud.

A few minutes later, Kate sits beside me. "That was dramatic," she says, taking one of my hands in hers. "You know I only care about you and want what's best?"

I don't feel like speaking, since I have nothing nice to say, so I just nod.

"Decker cares about you and wants what's best for you, too."

I yank my hand back. "Drop it."

She huffs. "Fine."

She starts filing her nails and I take the moment to change the subject. "So what's up with you? You've been acting weird lately."

She pauses in her task for a moment, then continues. "Nothing's up with me."

Right.

"You can play nonchalant all you want, but something's up with you." I grab the file out of her hand and start doing my own.

"I was using that," she whines.

"Start talking," I say.

She starts chewing the inside of her lip.

Kate's nervous!? Oooh, this is gonna be good.

"I've been talking to a guy," she finally says, so quietly I almost don't hear her.

"What?!" I ask, dropping the file and turning on the couch to face her. "Tell me everything!"

She rolls her eyes at my exuberance. "It's nothing," she says. "He's totally not my type."

I tip my head to the side. Kate has never indicated that she had a type, though I guess I'd always assumed he'd be a handsome, studious bookworm—like she is. Well, except for the handsome part. Women shouldn't be described as handsome. Maybe the guy would pre-med, like her, or pre-law even. Pre something.

"He rides a motorcycle. He's a mechanic." She says it so matter-of-factly and then just shrugs; my eyes widen. There's nothing negative about a motorcycle-riding mechanic, it's just not as clean-cut as the future doctor or lawyer I'd imagined in my head. "He came into the restaurant a couple months ago. We talked a little bit but he was there with his friends so we couldn't talk much. He gave me his number before he left, and we've sort of been texting ever since. Sometimes we talk on the phone."

Whoa.

I'm not even sure what information to tackle first. Kate, my roommate who has always been more introverted than me, has been talking to a guy, secretly, for months now. A guy who may be a bad boy. And she's blushing. *My* Kate is *blushing*!

"Say something!" she shrieks, slapping my arm. That kind of stung, chick's got strength. I rub the spot on my arm and scowl at her.

"You've been busy!"

If possible, her blush reddens even more, and it makes me laugh. "It's not like that," she says quietly.

"Then what's it like? Are you trying to tell me you guys aren't sexting?"

"Casey!" she exclaims, slapping my arm again.

"Ouch! What?"

"Stop it!"

"Not until you tell me more. Where does he work? What's he look like? I don't even know where to begin!" We've never had conversations like this before. We were both always single and focused on academics. It was the same for me in high school. Decker was the only guy in my life, and I'd never talked about him with Jane, and she was really my only female friend.

"He works at a repair shop in San Jose. He's tall, dark and handsome."

I roll my eyes at her generic description. "What's his name?"

She shakes her head at my obvious disapproval of the lack of details. "Jay."

I nod, unable to immediately come up with any serial killer's named Jay. "Do you like him?"

She looks down at her hands in her lap, and nods. "Yeah. But it's never going to be anything, so it doesn't matter."

I take her hand and nudge her to look at me. "Why would you think that? You're amazing, beautiful, smart..."

She laughs. "Yeah, but we're so different. He's totally hot, and he knows it. He and his friends are boisterous and out of control. He's my complete opposite."

"Hey, you're hot, too. And you know what they say, 'opposites attract.'"

"That's so cliché." She sighs and starts digging in her little bag of nail polish. She's putting up a good front, but I know better. I don't like seeing my friend so defeated.

"If it's meant to be, it'll be," I say with a smirk, making her laugh.

"Ha-ha." She pulls two colors out of the bag. "Passion Pink or Radiant Rose?"

I point to the brighter of the two pinks. "Look, if he doesn't appreciate what's right in front of him, that's his problem. You're a great catch and it's his loss."

"It's complicated, Case. I just don't know."

I narrow my eyes at her. "What aren't you telling me?"

"Nothing. I told you everything that's relevant." She starts painting her nails, obviously trying to put an end to the conversation.

"Kate?"

"Yeah?" she asks, not looking up.

"What aren't you telling me?" I repeat. After a few moments of her silence, I add "You really like this guy, don't you?"

She takes a deep breath and looks up at me. "More than I can even explain."

I nod in acceptance, "Okay. That's good. If you care about him, then he can't be a bad guy, right? You're an excellent judge of character." And she is, she really is. You'd think *she* was the psych major. "I'm sorry I jumped to conclusions."

She visibly relaxes. "Thank you. He's a really great guy."

I smile at her. "Good. He better take good care of you."

She frowns.

"What is it?"

Shaking her head, she says "It's nothing."

"Kate?"

She sighs. "Jay–"

We're interrupted by the front door banging open and Decker coming through carrying about ten grocery bags. I stand to help him, but quickly turn back to Kate and point at her.

"We're not finished here," I promise her.

"I figured," she says grudgingly, before gathering up her nail supplies and hurrying off to her room.

I look down the hall at her closed door for a minute, dying to know what she was about to tell me. Eventually, I follow the sounds of ruckus and head into the kitchen where Decker is standing at the table unloading the grocery bags.

"What the heck did you buy?"

He smiles that mischievous smile. "You'll see."

Chapter Twenty-Four

Decker

"I can't believe you made biscuits and gravy," Casey says in between moans of delicious delight. "And I can't believe how good it is," she adds, shoveling in another bite.

"Hey, now. Be nice." I scowl while pointing at her with my fork. "My mom taught me a few things in the kitchen."

"What other recipes do you have up your sleeve?"

"Have patience, little one. You'll find out soon enough." I reach over and pat her head in a placating manner, causing her to glare at me.

"Who knew? Decker Abrams can cook."

I sigh. I hate it when she starts with the "Decker Abrams" shit. I know she's mocking me when she says that. "Give it a rest, Case. Yes, I can cook. Had nothing better to do when I was holed up for a semester recovering from my shoulder injury."

She frowns and sadly looks down at her plate.

Shit. That may have come out ruder than I intended. "I'm sorry, Casey. The wound is still a little raw, I guess."

She meets my eyes, her brown eyes almost black. "No, I'm sorry Decker. That was really insensitive of me. I shouldn't be surprised that you know how to cook. Your mom and dad are great cooks. I should have known that would have rubbed off on you."

"That and I *am* awesome," I smirk at her. She rolls her eyes and laughs at my cockiness, picking her fork back up. Mission accomplished. I'd never liked seeing Casey sad.

"So can we take Route 66 home?" I ask after I eat my last biscuit.

"No, it's not the most direct route."

"So what?"

She looks up at me, and in a tone that clearly questions my intelligence, says "It's a very long drive, Decker."

"No shit," I say sarcastically as I lean back in my seat, the front two legs coming off the ground. "Come on, Casey. It'll be an adventure. When are you ever gonna get to road trip with your best friend again?"

She's playing with her food but I can tell she's thinking about it. I can almost hear the squeak of the wheels inside her head. Finally, she sets down her fork, pushes back her plate, and leans forward with her elbows on the table.

"I'll go on this adventure with you Decker–"

I don't want for her to finish, I jump from the table and hurry to her side, lifting her out of her seat and spinning her around. She laughs as she slaps my arm, begging me to put her down. I miss hearing her laugh. She doesn't laugh enough. She's so serious all the time. I finally set her down and she sways a little, her equilibrium off from the spinning.

"Under one condition," she finishes, poking me in the chest with her pale pink fingernail.

Nothing she says is going to dampen my excitement. "Name it."

"You have to map out the entire trip."

"Done!" I fist pump, and she giggles.

"And you have to tell my mom we're going to take longer getting home," she says with a grin.

"Hey, that's two conditions," I whine, pretending to be upset when I'm still high over the fact that she's coming home. I have to hand it to her, though, she's smooth. Her mom is not going to be happy I'm planning a detour that's going to prevent her from having her daughter back home as soon as possible. It's almost worth skipping the adventure. *Almost.* "Deal!"

Casey groans, then laughs and takes off running when I try to pick her up again. "Decker, stop it! You're such a big kid!" On the way to her bedroom, her laughter turns into the occasional shriek when my fingertips nearly make contact.

"Gotcha," I say as I wrap my arms around her and swing her down onto the bed. I straddle her legs and grab hold of her left hand first, then her right, and use one hand to hold them both above her head. We're both breathing heavily from the run, wide smiles on both our faces, maybe something else? Her eyes look darker.

I lean forward, reach down, and tickle the side of her ribs.

"Decker!" she shrieks, squirming in an attempt to get away from me.

I let go of her hands and use both of mine now, attacking both her sides at once. She's laughing, yelling, slapping, and crying.

"I'm gonna pee! You're gonna make me pee!"

~ 194 ~

And tickle torture is over.

I quickly roll off her and wave my hands towards the bathroom. She glares at me as she carefully rolls off the bed and gives me a wide berth as she side steps around the perimeter of the room to the bathroom. I laugh at her ridiculousness. It's been a while since we've had that much fun. Maybe even since before high school.

I lie back on her bed, folding my hands behind my head and staring at the ceiling. *No glow-in-the-dark stars here*, I think to myself. I consider surprising her with some one day while she's at work, but I don't want this place to become any more of a home to Casey. I want her back in South Carolina. Even if I have to wait until she graduates.

I hear the toilet flush, and a moment later she steps out of her bathroom. She pauses when she sees me lying on the bed, and her cheeks turn a little pink. I smile and pat the bed beside me. It surprises me when she smiles back and hops up right next to me, lying on her side, resting her cheek against my chest with her arm wrapped around my stomach.

Like so many times before.

"I missed you so much," I tell her, tipping my face forward just enough to kiss the top of her head.

"I missed you so much, too." She squeezes my body for emphasis.

Eventually we get up and clean the kitchen from dinner. There isn't too much since I'd cleaned as I'd cooked. Casey packs up the leftovers for Kate, since she's working the late shift at the restaurant tonight. What she doesn't eat, we'll probably have for lunch one day.

Once we're finished, she takes my hand and leads me back to her bedroom. She lies down and pats the bed where I'd been lying before. I lie down and she curls up into my side again. We talk for a couple hours about everything and nothing. I miss this. I miss the connection Casey and I have always shared. I miss hearing her voice. I miss her warmth. I miss everything.

Everything.

And that may be a problem.

Chapter Twenty-Five

Casey

I'm taking Decker to the Golden Gate Bridge today. He wanted to bike it, but that much cardio would probably kill me, so we're walking it instead. We park in a lot near Ghirardelli Square since I plan to surprise him with a stop at the famous chocolate shop at the end of the night and take the cable car up and through the city. He's so mesmerized by the bridge that he doesn't even notice the famous sign towering nearby.

"Aren't we going in the wrong direction?" Decker asks, pointing to the bridge in the distance behind us.

I tip my head back, close my eyes, and enjoy the morning breeze running through my hair. "I thought you might like the cable car."

"It's moving slower than my grandmother drives," he groans, tapping his feet incessantly. His white knuckle grip on the side rail says otherwise, but I let it go.

"Only because we're going uphill."

"So let me get this straight," he says after a minute. "There is a cable in the ground pulling this thing?"

I open my eyes and tip my head towards him, he grins a cheesy grin, and I can't help but smile back. "Sort of. There *is* a cable in the ground, and it's always moving. The trolley grabs and lets go of the cable as needed when it stops and goes and stuff. The cable pulls it uphill, and on flat ground I guess, but not when it's going downhill. When it's going downhill it releases it."

His eyes widen. "You mean to tell me that this hunk of metal is like a runaway train going downhill on *these* hills?" His point is emphasized by a cable car rushing by in the other direction. "You're trying to kill me, aren't you?" he narrows his eyes at me.

I laugh. "It's perfectly safe. And come on, aren't guys supposed to be adrenaline junkies or something? This is nothing."

He sits back in his seat, crosses his arms over his chest, and huffs. "Adrenaline junkies," he mumbles to himself.

I stifle another laugh. *What a baby!* I gently pat his leg. "Don't worry, the ride down takes no time at all."

His eyes widen as he glares at me, yet again. "Yeah, not making me feel better."

"Quit being such a baby." We switch cars near Nob Hill and Decker has my hand in a death grip the entire trek down Mason. I'm surprised he doesn't get down on his hands and knees and kiss the ground when we get off at the end. Maybe it was the crowd.

"You know it's not likely you're going to live that down, right?" I ask him as we take a cab to Presidio.

"I don't even know what you're talking about," he says, looking out his window towards the bay.

"You shrieked."

The cabbie snorts and Decker shoots him a look. "I did not shriek."

"Pretty sure the ringing in my left ear says otherwise."

He rolls his eyes, "Whatever. Stop being so dramatic."

I burst out laughing, nearly rolling over in my seat. "I'm dramatic," I say once I've calmed down, "right!"

"I'll deny it," he says, completely serious.

One look at his straight face has me in hysterics again.

"Go ahead, yuck it up." He says, and I'm pretty sure that, through my tears of pure joy, I see the corner of his mouth turn up. I straighten myself up and reach over to take his hand. He gives my hand a small squeeze and smiles at me. "I've really missed you, Case."

"I've missed you, too, Deck."

***

"This is the most amazing thing I've ever seen in my life."

I sneak a peek at Decker. His eyes are bright and all his earlier stress completely gone. He turns in a complete circle, taking in the scene around him, and I laugh. He's just too much.

"Would you like a sample?" a young girl in the Ghirardelli uniform asks.

"You give samples?" Decker asks with the glee of a five-year-old.

The clerk smiles, "Sure. I have here dark chocolate with sea salt or milk chocolate and caramel."

Decker glances quickly at me, then back at the girl. "Can I have both?" He presses his palms together and holds them up in front of him. "Please?"

"Oh, dear lord, Decker." I shake my head, grab a milk chocolate and caramel, thank the clerk and walk away. I cannot watch a grown man beg for chocolate. Though I'm not sure what I expected bringing him here. The things Decker will do for chocolate...

Decker finds me several minutes later checking out the various ice cream flavors and toppings. "What? Did you buy the entire store?" I ask, gesturing to his two bags full of chocolate.

He gives me a "don't mess with me look" and proceeds to tell me all the flavors he bought and the great deal Heather, that's the clerk, gave him. I tried to explain to him that the offer was for all customers, but he insisted that it was his southern charm.

"I can't believe they have ice cream here, too. This place is amazing! Now I see why you like it here."

I laugh. "Yes, *this* is why I stay in California."

"You gonna get a sundae?" he says after looking at the menu board for a few minutes.

"I'm thinking about it."

He rubs his hands together in front of himself. "You get the banana split and I'll get the hot fudge brownie sundae."

I nod my head. "So, really, you want both and can't decide between the two?"

He smiles that devilish smile. "You know, there's a reason you're my best friend."

"If I recall, I didn't have much of a choice in the matter. I believe you *told* me I was going to be your best friend and that was that."

"Worked, didn't it?" he smirks and bumps my shoulder with his.

It sure did. How I lived three years without this guy, I'll never know. And now it's only going to be more difficult letting him go.

Chapter Twenty-Six

Decker

I had the most amazing time with Casey today. I'll give her one thing, the city *is* beautiful. It doesn't charm me the way home does, but the bridge, and the view from it, was gorgeous. I loved being able to see Alcatraz and wished we could have toured it. Maybe another day I'll be able to channel my inner Sean Connery and make that island my bitch. I feel like I need to make something my bitch after screaming like one on the cable car. That shit's not right.

Tonight we're doing pizza and a movie. Casey's roommate is out at work or something, so she and I take over the living room with our feast.

"Want a beer?" I ask her from the fridge.

"No, thanks."

"Beer not good enough for you?" I tease. I love giving her a hard time by suggesting she's a snobby wine drinker now that she's been in California.

"Ha-ha," she says dryly as she loads a couple slices of pepperoni pizza on her plate. "I don't even know how I'm going to eat this after all that ice cream."

"We can always have the leftovers for lunch tomorrow," I offer. "Or breakfast."

"Ew," she scrunches up her nose. "I don't understand how you can eat pizza for breakfast."

I laugh. "It's not like I invented the concept. Plenty of people do it."

"Whatever. It's gross. Breakfast food is delicious. I could eat breakfast food all day long."

"I can't argue with that," I agree.

"That's because you could eat *anything* all day long. Of course you can't argue with that."

"Truth," I mumble through a mouthful of pizza.

"You're so gross," she says, shaking her head at me.

"But you love me anyway."

"I do," she nods, completely matter of fact.

"So, I was thinking."

"Uh-oh," she interrupts.

"Shut up." I throw a piece of pepperoni at her which she effortlessly, and surprisingly, catches in her mouth.

She waves off my applause. "I'm talented, what can I say?"

"Apparently. As I was saying before I was so rudely interrupted...I was thinking that when we get home, we could go out with the old crew from high school." I don't really want to share Casey with any of them, except maybe Sam, but since part of the demise of our friendship had been due to the fact that I'd never included her when I'd hung out with them, this may be a positive step.

I eye her carefully as she pauses in sipping her drink. "I didn't have a crew in high school."

"The guys always liked you."

"Right," she says dryly.

"They did," I argue.

"Look, Decker, just because I'm going to be home for the summer, doesn't mean you have to entertain me. I'll be just fine by myself. I always was." She said the last part so quietly, I almost didn't hear her.

"I'm trying to make an effort here and you're making it really difficult."

"I don't want to fight, Deck. Can we just watch the movie?" Her voice has lost its edge and she just sounds tired.

But I'm not ready to let it go. I pick up the remote and press pause. "No. Why don't you like my friends?"

She sighs and sets her plate and cup on the coffee table. "I don't have a problem with your friends."

"Bullshit. If you didn't have a problem with them then you wouldn't have a problem hanging out with them." I'm not sure why I'm getting defensive, I don't even really want to hang out with anyone from high school—not when I can be with her, but it pisses me off when Casey's not honest with me. And right now I know she's not telling the truth. About this and who knows what else.

"Jeez, Decker!" she slaps her hands down against her thighs. "*I* don't have a problem with your friends. *They* have a problem with *me*."

"What? No. They never had a problem when you tagged along." She shoots me a glare when I say "tagged along." "I didn't mean it like that," I say, raising my hands in what I hope will come off as a gesture of surrender and not piss her off more.

"That's just it, Deck," she says sadly. "I did tag along. And that's how they all saw it. They tolerated me, the geeky girl, because of you. But they weren't always that kind to me."

"What do you mean?" I ask, feeling my face heat up at the thought of my friends being mean to Casey.

"They made fun of me, Deck. Never while you're around, of course. But in the hallway at school and in gym. The girls only ever tried to get close to me because I was close to you, but they never liked me. They said some mean stuff."

I stand up and start to pace. "What did they say?"

"It's no big deal. It's old news," she says, waving her hand dismissively before she gets up and starts cleaning up the pizza buffet from the coffee table.

"It *is* a big deal and since I'm only just now finding out about it, it's *not* old news. What. Did. They. Say?" I emphasize each word so she knows I'm not kidding around.

I help her bring the pizza and plates into the kitchen. Then take her hand and lead her back to the couch. We sit down, and I squeeze her hand. "Tell me. Please."

She takes a deep breath and looks up at me. "There wasn't ever really one thing. Like they didn't have a nickname for me or anything, though the most common was 'Decker's Shadow.'" I start to stand up, but she tugs me back down. "If you expect me to tell you then you need to chill out. It was a long time ago, I'm over it."

"Yeah but you shouldn't have had to deal with it in the first place. And why the hell didn't you tell me?"

She shrugs like it's no big deal. It *is* a big deal. A very big deal. I would have done anything for her back then. I still would. And to think my friends, and I use that term loosely, were talking shit about her behind my back. It pisses me the fuck off.

"What else?" I ask through gritted teeth.

"When the girls weren't trying to use me to get closer to you, they'd just taunt me. Saying things like you'd never be interested in a nerd like me, or they couldn't understand how you'd want to spend time with someone like me."

I shake my head...unbelievable. I knew the girls I hung out with in high school were shallow and superficial, but I had no idea they were being mean to Casey. And they couldn't understand why I'd want to spend time with Casey? Maybe because she was the most amazing girl in the world...still is.

"And the guys?" I ask, almost not wanting to know.

"They just said some crude things."

My fists clench, and I don't realize I'm squeezing Casey's hand until she shakes mine off. "Sorry," I say, frowning. "What did they say?" These guys had been like brothers to me, my teammates. I'd trusted them.

"They said stuff about how I wasn't much to look at, but I must have been good in bed for you to hang around me so much."

I let out an animalistic growl and stand up, pulling at my hair with my hands. I can't believe this shit! It makes me sick that I spent time with those assholes, not knowing what was going on behind my back. That they were saying such awful thing about the most important person in my life.

"What the fuck, Casey? And you didn't think I deserved to know that?! I was with those assholes all the time! I would have kicked their fucking asses!"

She's quiet and when I turn around in see that she has her head in her hands and her shoulders are shaking.

She's crying.

Damn it!

I rush over to the couch and kneel down in front of her. "Casey, baby, you know that's all bullshit. Don't let the stupid shit those guys said make you feel this way. You're so much stronger than that. You're the best girl I know. Then and now. I'm sorry I yelled at you. It's not your fault."

She looks up at me with tear-soaked eyes. "It *is* my fault, Decker. I knew better," she cried.

She *knew* better? "Casey," I say, tipping up her chin to look at me. "What do you mean? What are you talking about?"

She shakes her head and drops her chin back down to her chest. "You hear something too many times," she whispers, "you start to believe it's true."

My brow furrows in confusion. "Believe what's true? Casey, you didn't actually think I felt that way about you? Did you?"

She shrugs. "I didn't really know what to think, Decker. My self-esteem wasn't all that great from being picked on all the time. And you never wanted to bring me out with your friends."

"Because they were immature! You were too good for them! We talked about that!"

"In retrospect I can see that, but at the time it hurt."

"Is that what made you leave?"

She stood from the couch and started pacing. "No. Maybe. I don't know. We talked about this at the dock, do we have to rehash it?"

I stand up and get in her way so she has to stop and look at me. "We talked about some stuff at the dock, but you didn't tell me how they'd acted towards you. You didn't tell me that you believed the shit they said. Do you really think that little of me?"

"I was a hormonal teenage girl, Decker. An outcast. And you were like the hottest guy in school. You were with me, almost every night, and I couldn't fathom why. The guys would stay that stuff, and I wondered if you were running off to them every morning to laugh at my expense since you were never there when I woke up."

I place my hands on her shoulders. "Casey, I never ran off and told anyone about us. And before you start jumping to conclusions, it's not because I was ashamed of you. It's because what was between us was between us. The only reason I was never there in the morning is because I was terrified your parents would catch me in there. Simple as that. I would have stayed in bed with you all damn day if I could have." And that was the damn truth. Being with Casey was the only time I ever felt complete.

I finally feel some of the tension leaving her shoulders. She takes a step towards me and rests her head against my chest. I lower my arms from her shoulders and wrap them around her, pulling her in tight.

"If that's all true, why didn't you ever want to date me?"

I did want to date you, damn it. But you were my best friend, and I was terrified my dumbass would do something stupid and lose you forever. Just like I did anyway.

I breathe in the lingering scent of her shampoo. Sweet and citrusy. "Because I was an idiot? I didn't think you thought about us that way."

"I was a girl, Decker. Of course I thought about us that way." She sniffles, and it breaks my heart.

"I wish you'd told me." Things could have been so different. Not that it's either of our faults; we were just kids. We still are.

"I'm so sorry, Decker. All of the misunderstandings. All of my stupid fears. All of that wasted time. I'm sorry."

"It's alright, babe." I rub soothing circles on her back. She always liked that when she was upset or not feeling well. "We've got plenty of time to make up for it."

She sniffles again and squeezes me tighter, as if she doesn't want to let go. Truth is, I don't want her to. I sure don't want to let her go. But I don't want to freak her out either, and it seems like any time I get too close, she takes ten steps back.

"How about we watch that movie now?" I ask, nodding towards the television.

Casey pulls away from me and wipes her eyes. "That sounds good." She smiles shyly at me and I tug her back to the couch. She cuddles back into my side and sighs contentedly.

Being with her like this...it feels almost too good to be true.

Chapter Twenty-Seven

Casey

The bass is thumping so loud I feel like my head is about to explode. I can't believe I let Decker talk me into going to a club. A club! I am barely a bar person, let alone a club person. I reach behind me to grab Kate's hand. Yep, I'm that friend. If I am being forced out of my comfort zone and into a club, so is my roommate, who is even further out of her comfort zone than I am.

"I need to get some air," I shout to her over the music.

She nods that she heard me and stays put, knowing that Decker will be back any minute with our drinks and if we're not right where he left us, he'll freak out. Who am I kidding? He's going to freak out when he gets back, and I'm not there anyway.

I step out onto the back deck of the club and the chill of the night air immediately causes goosebumps to pepper my skin. I cross my arms and rub my upper arms for warmth. I don't exactly keep club clothes around the apartment, and neither does Kate, so I improvised with the shortest black skirt I had—which still ended just a little above my knees—and white tank top. I look like I've just let my hair down after a long board meeting, not like a clubber. Oh well, I'm over what other people think of me.

I look around the deck and there only a handful of people out here. A couple is making out in one of the dark corners, a couple girls are smoking at one of the picnic tables, and on the far side a guy is talking on his cell phone.

I step over to the wooden railing and lean forward on my forearms, looking out onto the bay. Decker found this place one day during his travels. I had no idea it was even here. Had no reason to know, or find out for that matter. It's not a bad place, just loud. So not my thing. But I need to learn to live a little, right?

I'm standing there, taking in the bay, when I feel heat behind me. *Decker.* I feel warmth against my back as he leans forward, pressing against me. But I instantly tense when two tattooed forearms appear on the railing on both sides of me. Decker doesn't have tattoos. I straighten up quickly, accidentally smacking the back of my head into the guy's face, causing him to grunt. I spin around quickly, taking in the aggressor.

"What the fuck?" he calls out, keeping his hands coned over his nose. He's taller than me, which isn't too difficult to accomplish, but he's thin, lanky. *Decker can take him,* I think to myself.

"Maybe you should try not startling women, and you wouldn't get hurt," I tell him, crossing my arms over my chest and popping my hip out to the side.

"Crazy bitch," he says.

I'm starting to get a little nervous because I'm sort of in the corner of the deck, and he's blocking my path to the back door. *Why won't he just leave?* "Look, I'm really sorry. I didn't mean to hurt you. You startled me, and I jumped."

The guy stands up straight, finally lowering his hands from his face, and glares at me. His eyes are dark, soulless. There is blood running from his nose and his face is already starting to bruise. I wince and take a step back, which puts me right against the railing. I feel trapped, and my body tenses.

Smooth, Casey. Why didn't you just run when he was bent over? Could have at least gotten out of this damn corner.

I look around, noticing for the first time that we're alone on the deck. The couple in the opposite corner are gone, as are the smokers and the guy on his cell phone. Or maybe is this cell phone guy—I hadn't gotten a good look.

Shit.

"Look, I said I was sorry." *Think, Casey, think!* "My boyfriend is going to be outside with my drink any second. It'll probably be best if you're not here when he comes."

He laughs, it's a maniacal sound that makes me cringe. This is why I don't go out. There are far better ways to die, more dignified ways, than by a crazy ass goon at a damn night club.

Why didn't I take that damn self-defense class with Kate?

He takes a step forward and reaches his hand out to touch my cheek, but before he makes contact, I hear the most beautiful sound in the world.

"There you are." Decker slips in between me and the goon and looks into my eyes with a concerned green gaze. He holds my face between his hands and seems to give my soul a thorough examination through my eyes.

I smile and can see some of the tension leave his body. He turns to look at the goon and winces, probably at the blood. "Thanks for keeping my girl company," he says amicably as he puts his arm around my shoulder and pulls me into his side. My heart flutters at his words and the gesture, though I know he's just playing a part to get us out of this mess.

The goon seems to be sizing Decker up, and must realize that he's no match, because he simply shrugs and says "no problem" before turning around and exiting the deck to the street. I let out a breath I hadn't realized I'd been holding.

Decker quickly turns to me. "Are you okay?" He holds my face in his hands again; his eyes scanning me from head to toe for any harm.

"I'm fine," I try to assure him. It doesn't work.

"What the fuck happened? I leave you for five minutes! Why didn't you just stay inside where I could see you?" He runs his hands through his hair, a nervous gesture I'm familiar with—or at least I used to be.

"I came out for air. He approached me from behind and startled me, I jumped and the back of my head might have broken his nose." I cringe on that last part.

Decker stares at me for a minute, then laughs. "You accidentally broke the guy's nose with your head?"

I shrug. "What can I say? I'm badass like that."

He continues to laugh as he takes my hand and leads me inside. "Come on, Kate's watching our drinks. I think her boyfriend just showed up."

"Jay?" I ask, curious. I didn't expect to meet him this quickly. Can't say I'm not thrilled though.

"Yeah, I think that's what she said his name was. It was pretty loud, though." He pauses at the door and turns to look me in the eyes. "You sure you're okay?"

I roll my eyes. "I'm fine." Protective Decker is in the house.

"Because we can go home if you want to."

"No, it's okay. I'm completely fine. Plus, I want to meet Jay." If Jay hadn't shown up, I would have been all over Decker's offer to go home. Now, I need to meet the guy who has my roommate all kinds of frazzled.

He nods. "As long as you're good."

I squeeze his hand. "I'm safe with you, Decker." He beams at me, then tucks me into his side. I feel warm all over, and it's not from the little bit of alcohol I'd had. It's from Decker.

When he opens the door, the noise level seems even more elevated from being outside in the quiet for so long. Decker grips my hand tightly, keeping me right behind him, as he leads me back to Kate. When we finally get to the high top table, Kate's alone.

"Decker said Jay was here," I call out, totally disappointed.

She nods and leans across the table so she doesn't have to shout quite as loud. "He's here with some friends. Just went to get another drink."

I smile and nod as she shakes her head. She knows I'm looking forward to getting the opportunity to size him up. She gives me a look, one that begs me not to embarrass her. I wink back. I will neither confirm nor deny my intentions.

Chapter Twenty-Eight

Decker

Casey and I have a pretty good buzz going. We've had a few drinks, but we've been dancing them off. I had absolutely no idea the girl could move, but damn. Watching her hips sway from side to side and having her rub up against me is bringing back memories. Some of my favorite memories.

Hell. Who am I kidding? All my favorite memories include Casey. The times I shared with her, in the bedroom and out, were better than baseball. Yeah, I said it.

"I'm gonna get some water," I say, leaning in to speak in her ear. She nods that she heard me and keeps dancing with Kate.

I go back to our table, which Jay and his friends are guarding. I don't know what's going on between him and Kate, but I'm pretty sure he looks at her the way I look at Casey. Like she hung the moon and all the stars.

"Hey, man." I nod as I grab an unopened bottle of water, twist the cap off, and chug.

"So what's up with you and Casey?" he asks after I set the empty bottle down.

"What's up with you and Kate?" I counter.

He smirks. "Kate says you two are 'just friends,' but I see the way you look at her." For a badass looking dude with more muscles than me and a shitload of tattoos, he sure seems to wax poetic.

I shrug. "She's my best friend. Has been my whole life."

Now he laughs. *What the fuck?* "Kate says you two only just recently reconnected after being apart for a few years."

"Yeah, so?" *Jesus, Is there anything Kate hasn't told him?*

"Does she know you're in love with her?"

My eyes widen and I choke on my last swallow of water. "Excuse me?" I look around at his friends, but they're involved in their own conversations and not paying any attention to us.

"She's special, yeah?"

My eyes find Casey on the dance floor, and I can feel my face light up.

I nod in response to Jay's question. "She's everything."

***

Much to Casey's surprise, and mine if I'm being honest, Kate decides to go home with Jay after the club so we have the apartment to ourselves. I'm in the kitchen fixing us a nightcap while Casey is in her bedroom changing. I'm trying not to think about her naked in the other room. But it's hard. Physically and literally.

Suddenly I feel her tiny arms wind their way around my chest. "Whatcha doin' handsome?"

Okay, so she's still a little buzzed. And I can't say that feeling her hot little body pressed up against my back doesn't feel heavenly.

"Fixing you some tea," I tell her, after regaining my composure. "Blueberry something or other." I turn around in her arms and she beams up at me. *Ugh.* Feeling her pressed up against the front of my body is so much better.

"Thank you, Decker. You take such good care of me."

I smile back. "I always will."

Her smile falters slightly as she takes the mug from me. "Let's watch some TV in my room."

I grab my hot chocolate—don't judge—and dutifully follow her down the short hall to her room. She's wearing these tiny pink and white striped pajamas and it's really difficult to think straight.

"Decker?"

"Huh?"

She laughs over her shoulder. "I asked what you want to watch."

I shrug. "Whatever you want is fine."

"Desperate Housewives?"

"Hell no!" What the crap is wrong with her?

She laughs. "Just checking to see if you were paying attention."

"Sorry, still a little buzzed I guess." A half-truth. I *am* a little buzzed on the alcohol, but I'm mostly high on her.

I set my mug on the nightstand and flop down on the bed, resting my head on her pillow. It smells just like her. Sweet. Sexy. Casey.

She sets her mug down beside mine and crawls across me, rubbing her breasts and pelvis against me as she goes. Evil woman. Once she's settled beside me, she sneaks a peek up at me. Her big, innocent brown eyes boring into mine.

She knows exactly what she's doing. The little shit. Well, two can play that game.

I smile down at her. "Mind if I get more comfortable?" She shakes her head in the negative and I stand from the bed. She quickly hustles underneath the covers as I take off my shirt and jeans, leaving me in only form-fitting boxer briefs.

She bites her bottom lip as I get into bed beside her and underneath the covers. I reach my hand up to her face and rub my thumb across her bottom lip, breaking it free of the confines of her teeth. I smirk and lean back down against the pillow, laughing to myself as she huffs.

She has on the Game Show Network and an old episode of *Family Feud* is on. We're calling out answers and laughing at some of the things the contestants are coming up with when I suddenly feel her leg against mine.

I hope she doesn't hear my sharp intake of breath, but judging by the fact that she starts running her foot up and down my leg, I'm certain she did. I school my expression, waiting to see how this plays out.

Does she want me as badly as I want her? It's been almost three years since I've felt her in an intimate way and memories of the delicious sensations are making it hard to resist rolling over and claiming her right now.

Apparently the same cannot be said for Casey, because all of a sudden she's on me. *She* takes *my* mouth in a punishing kiss, and I'm stunned before quickly coming to my senses.

I raise my arms to her sides, slipping them beneath her little tank top and feeling her skin. I suck her bottom lip into my mouth as I slowly raise her top.

She pulls back and shakes her head. "Shirt stays on," she whispers quickly before falling back on my mouth. Our tongues are intertwined in an intense, passionate, crazy dance.

God she tastes so good.

I run my hands down her body and grab her ass, holding on tight as I flip us over. Her legs spread apart, and I rest between them, thrusting myself against her.

She feels so good, too.

"Oh...*Decker*...that feels so good," she moans out, grinding against my thrusts.

Jesus, I feel like a virgin again, ready to blow, and we've both still got our clothes on. I pull back and look into her eyes. They are clear, not the slightest bit of hesitation in their chocolate depths.

She reaches down to the waistband of my boxers and pushes the right side down over my hip.

~ 226 ~

"Are you sure?" I ask her, still looking into her eyes for any hint of indecision or drunkenness, but all I see is clarity, desire and longing.

She nods desperately and continues to push my shorts down, bending her knees and using her feet to bring them the rest of the way. I lean forward and take her lips again, licking and sucking, first the upper then the lower...hoping to convey everything I am feeling in that one connection.

She's it for me. It's always been Casey. It'll always be her.

I kiss a trail down her cheek, then her neck, quickly moving over the clothed portion of her body. I make a mental note to ask her what that's about later—it's not like it's anything I haven't already seen. But I don't want to ruin this moment with talking. We can talk later.

Using both hands, I grip the waistband of her pajama shorts and pull them and her panties down in one swoop. I lean in and place a kiss just below her naval, but before I can go any lower she grabs me by my biceps and pulls me up.

"Make love to me, Decker," she begs into my mouth.

I look into her eyes again, still as clear and beautiful as ever. "No regrets?"

She shakes her head. "Never," she promises me.

"Shit," I pause, pulling away.

She grabs on to my arms and pulls me closer. "What is it?"

"I need a condom," I say, pulling away again.

"I'm safe. I'm on the pill. I'm safe, Decker. Please. Please just make love to me." There is a quiet desperation in her voice, and her eyes are wild. With passion? With want?

I frame her face in my hands and kiss her, massaging her tongue with mine. "I love you, Casey. I love you so damn much," I confess as I thrust inside her.

I'm home.

Casey's my home. Always has been, always will be.

Chapter Twenty-Nine

Casey

I wake up and stretch, deliciously sore from the previous night's activities. Decker and I made love all night long. I grin as the memories run through my mind. That's exactly what it was—love. He told me as much.

I should have returned the sentiment—I wanted to. I feel it. I've always felt it. But I couldn't. Not when this is going to have to end. Regret begins to swirl deep in my gut.

How could I be so stupid? This is only going to make everything that much worse! For both of us, but him especially.

I roll over to face Decker. He is so beautiful, so peaceful. I haven't seen him look this calm, even in sleep, since we've reunited. He's lying on his back, a few of his long hairs lay haphazardly over his forehead. His lashes rest on his cheeks, which are still a little flush with color.

I reach my arm over and gently brush his hair off his forehead, running my fingers down the side of his face. The corners of his mouth tip up, and I know he's awake.

"Good morning, gorgeous," he says in his sleep-sexy voice that makes my whole body tremble.

I look past him to the nightstand and see that it's just after noon. "More like afternoon," I correct.

He looks over at the clock, eyes wide. "Wow, I haven't slept this late in a long time."

"Me neither."

"I guess we did only go to bed a few hours ago," he smirks and winks.

I feel my cheeks heat and try to roll away, but he's too quick. He rolls over and reaches out with his long arm to hook me back in. Now we're lying on our sides, my back to his front. Still naked.

"Um, Decker?"

"Um, Casey?"

I lightly nudge him with my elbow. "Don't you think we should get up?"

"Nah," he says, pulling me in tighter. "I think it would be perfectly fine if we stay here like this forever."

I sigh. My mind is warring against itself. On one hand, Decker is absolutely right. It would be perfectly fine if we stay like this forever. On the other hand, reality bites. We can't stay here forever. Not even close.

"I have to pee," I say, wriggling free of his grasp.

"Hurry back!"

***

I manage to escape falling back into bed with Decker by claiming I need to refuel. He's a guy, so he buys it. I head to the kitchen to scavenge for breakfast. I haven't shopped for groceries since I've been back so I'm hoping Kate has something since Decker and I have been doing a lot of dining out.

I hear a noise from the back of the apartment and realize Decker must be finally getting out of bed. I snatch up a blueberry yogurt from the back of the fridge and check the date. Satisfied I'm not going to get sick, I grab a spoon and take a seat at the table. I peel off the lid and take in one heavenly spoonful.

Mmm, sustenance.

Decker starts the shower and I freeze. That's not close enough to be the bathroom he's supposed to be sharing with Kate. He's in *my* bathroom.

Shit.

Shit. Shit. Shit.

I drop the yogurt, not caring if it spills out on the table, and run from the kitchen to my bedroom. Sure enough, the bathroom door is closed and the shower is running.

Fuck!

I reach for the handle. Locked. Dammit! Since when do guys lock the bathroom door? I bang on the door. "Decker!"

"Yeah," he calls out. His voice muffled by the sounds of the shower.

"I told you to use Kate's bathroom," I say. Yeah, I realize how lame I sound.

"Sorry, I didn't think you'd mind. I just jumped in after I used the bathroom." Damn him for having such a reasonable explanation. Of course he'd have a reasonable explanation, though. It's just a shower. Just a shower in a bathroom that happens to hold many of my secrets.

"Why'd you lock the door?"

"Habit, I guess. Sharing a dorm with guys, if you weren't careful they'd just barge in. Some of them have no boundaries at all."

"Present company included," I mumble quiet enough that he can't hear.

"What's the big deal? We used to take baths together for crying out loud."

"We were six! And in bathing suits!" Unbelievable.

"You're overreacting, Case. I'll be out in a second."

I sigh, my heart racing in my chest. If he sees...he can't. He just can't. I take a few steps back until the back of my legs hit my bed, then I lower myself down. I can't take my eyes off the bathroom door. My ears are tuned in to every sound behind it.

Finally, the water cuts off and I hear the screech of the shower curtain moving along the rod. *Hurry up, Decker!* I hear quiet sounds that are probably him drying himself off with the towel. My knee bounces.

"Case?" he calls out.

"Yes?" I croak.

"Do you have any q-tips?"

My heart stops.

"No!" I shout, just as I hear the click of the medicine cabinet opening. I jump up and run for the door, knowing damn well it is still locked, but hoping, just hoping, he grants me some kind of mercy and has already unlocked it.

Still locked.

Shit.

It's silent—dead silent—on the other side of the door. I lean my head on the wood and exhale. I know he's seen what's inside. He wouldn't be so damn quiet otherwise.

Finally...finally I hear him disengage the lock. I take a step back and look up when he opens it. My heart breaks at the stricken look on his face. As much as I want to let my eyes roam down his beautifully toned body, with water droplets running right down his muscular chest and stomach and disappearing into the towel wrapped around his waist, I don't. I keep my eyes in line with his.

"Case, what's going on?" he asks, his voice barely a whisper, but skeptical. He's scared or nervous—maybe both. Confused, too. Definitely confused.

I will myself not to cry. I'd never wanted Decker to see this side of me. I'd never wanted him to know about any of it. I didn't want him to worry or be sad. I didn't want to break his heart the way the news broke mine.

I steel myself, doing what I do best. Keeping people out. Pushing people away. My parents. Decker. I'd do it to Kate, too, if I didn't live with her.

I turn off my emotions. Shut myself down. I'm a pro at this. One would have to be to live with the hand I've been dealt, otherwise you'd spend your days and nights in tears...feeling sorry for yourself.

With my armor on, I tell him "It's nothing. You should probably just go, Decker."

"Bullshit it's nothing!" he shouts. Pointing back to the bathroom he says, "You have more medicine bottles in that cabinet than a goddamn pharmacy, and you're going to tell me it's nothing?"

Like the coward that I am I turn away from him. I've never had to put this armor on for Decker before. It's not as easy with him. "Leave." My voice is flat, firm, though there was a slight crack I pray he didn't notice.

"Casey–"

"Just go!" *Don't go.* I don't want him to go, not really. But he needs to. I can't do this with him. I can't do this *to* him. He needs to leave before things get worse.

"No!" He grabs my shoulder and spins me around. He places a hand on each shoulder, holding me in place, and looks me straight in the eyes. "I am not leaving. You are not pushing me away. What the fuck is going on? What is all that? You're sick? Is this why haven't come home? Talk to me, Casey, because I'm freaking the fuck out right now!"

His eyes are wild, crazy. They're their brightest green and glassy, like he may break down and cry at any moment. I feel the pressure in the back of my eyes from my own tears wanting to break free. The lump rises in my throat. I could just open my mouth, and in a few words explain all this away. I could do that.

But I'm a coward.

A big, fat, stupid coward.

"Decker, you need to leave. Now!" I step back and break his hold on me, then lift my hands and push against his chest so he stumbles out of my bedroom doorway and into the hall. "Go!"

"Casey?" he pleads, and his voice cracks. "Please don't do this. Talk to me, baby. Please?"

"I'm not your baby," I tell him, never breaking eye contact...breaking his heart instead. It's the only way he'll leave. It's the only way I won't completely break his soul later on.

"Where the hell am I supposed to go?" A few tears have managed to escape his eyes, and I follow their trail down his cheeks. The cheeks that, not long ago, were freshly flushed from our night of passion.

"Home," I say flatly and then shut my bedroom door. Locking Decker out. Out of my life, but never out of my heart. He'd engrained himself in there so deeply fifteen years ago that he's never coming out.

"Casey!" he bangs on the door. "You're supposed to be going home with me. We can talk about this. Please. Please!"

I curl up on my bed and hug my pillow to my chest. It smells like Decker. I lift it up to my face to stifle the sound of the first sob. Decker is still banging on the door and yelling, so he probably wouldn't be able to hear me anyway, but I don't take any chances. I completely give in to the sadness, the devastation of losing my best friend again, and cry.

I cry for Decker because I'm not sure he'll ever forgive me for this. Especially now.

I cry for my mom and dad because they're the best parents a girl could ever have and I miss my dad so damn much.

I cry for Kate for having to put up with my sorry ass.

I cry for me because, let's face it, my life sucks.

And I cry for my broken heart...because if it had never broken in the first place, things might have been so much different.

I cry until I can no longer hear Decker at my door.

...until the sun goes down.

...until everything fades to black.

Chapter Thirty

Decker

I aimlessly walk around the apartment complex for a while, then head down the street to a little diner Casey and I went to for lunch one day. I have absolutely no idea what had just happened. No idea. Things were fine. They were great. She was opening up. At least I'd thought she was.

Then the pills. God...there'd been so many of them. With names I couldn't even pronounce, let alone remember. Is she sick? She's got to be with that many little orange bottles. But with what? How can she keep it from me?

I think back over the days we'd spent together both here and back home, and I can't recall any different or careful behaviors that would suggest she wasn't well. She'd gone fishing, she drank alcohol, she ate a little bit of everything and she ate it a lot. Yeah, she'd looked pretty sickly when she first showed up, but I hadn't really given it a second thought once I'd realized her father died, and she'd just driven cross-country on very little sleep.

I want to call my mom. I want to call Casey's mom. Surely they know what is going on—and don't even get me started on how pissed I am that they've hidden it from me. But I left my damn cell phone in the apartment. So that confrontation will have to wait.

I'm not leaving California without Casey. Not a damn chance. Especially now that I know something's wrong with her. I'll give her space...for now...but I'm not leaving her. When she came home a few short weeks ago, I said I wasn't letting her go again and I meant it. Whatever this shit is, she'll get through it with me right by her side. The way it was always supposed to be.

The bell rings as I enter the diner. I slide into one of the retro style booths and ask the waitress for a coffee. It's pretty dead, so I hope she won't mind if I just hang out here for a while. I need to give Casey her space, and I need to think.

She'd passed out that day when she'd had her blood drawn. Does that have something to do with this? Whatever *this* is? Did her being sick cause her pass out? Or is that why she'd had to have blood drawn? I can't believe she's been hiding this. Easy enough when she's across the country playing the avoidance game, but I've been right here. Right here!

I can't believe my parents didn't tell me. They had to have known she was sick all along. They're best friends with Casey's parents. There is no way Casey's parents wouldn't have told them. Why wouldn't they have told me? Why keep something like this from me? All of them...Casey included. I get she was upset with me when she left Charleston, but her health is bigger than that. At least it is to me.

I thank the waitress when she sets the mug in front of me, along with a bowl of cream and sugar packets. I should have told her I drink it black. I take a sip, and the hot liquid burns my insides, but it still doesn't suppress the pain I feel from being lied to and pushed aside, yet again, by the one girl I'd give my life for. The girl who owns my heart and soul. The girl who always has. Since she was six years old.

I was standing at the window in the front of our new house, looking out at the girl in the white dress with the brown hair.

"Momma, is that an angel?" I asked my mom with awe as she walked into the living room carrying another box.

My mom laughed at me. "That's just the little girl who lives across the street."

I kept watching her in amazement. She was smiling and dancing around. She seemed so happy all by herself in her imaginary world.

My mom knelt down beside me. "Why don't you go say 'hi' to her? Make a new friend," she said, nudging me towards the door.

I looked at her like she was crazy. "But she's a girl."

She laughed at me again. "Boys and girls can be friends, Decker."

I look back out at the girl in the white dress. I did want to be her friend. I wanted to be her best friend.

I'm brought back to the present by the waitress asking if I want a refill. I nod and thank her. Only an hour has passed. In my experience with Casey, she needs at least three to cool down. I grab a magazine off a neighboring table and flip through the pages to pass the time.

***

Two hours later, I'm sitting on the ground outside the apartment door, my forearms resting on top of my knees. I knocked, but there was no answer. Casey's car is in the

~ 241 ~

parking lot, but not Kate's. I have a key, but if Casey is in there and doesn't want to see me, I don't want to violate her privacy by barging in. I'm hoping one of them eventually turns up and puts me out of my misery.

I'm sort of hoping that it's Kate because I have a feeling she'll cave and tell me what's going on with Case. One thing I've realized about the new Casey is that when she builds walls, they're damn near impenetrable.

I lay my head back against the siding, thinking back to the good times Casey and I had shared growing up.

"Decker, that was amazing!" Casey called out, running up to me as I walked out of the dugout.

"Thanks," I said. My team won, but I was pretty bummed that I got struck out in the last inning.

"It was so cool seeing you out there throwing the ball! Just like the guys on TV." It was my first Little League game, and Casey's first baseball game ever. Her enthusiasm was pretty contagious, and I found myself smiling along with her.

"It was pretty cool," I admitted.

"So cool," she smiled. "I'm gonna come to every single one of your games. I told my dad I wanted to, and he said it was okay."

I grinned at her. "You're gonna come to every single one of my games?"

~ 242 ~

"Of course! You're my best friend. I wouldn't miss 'em for the world!"

And she hadn't missed a single game. She'd been there through Little League, middle school, junior high, and high school. Casey had gone to every game with my parents, home or away. Day or night, rain or shine.

Casey had always been there for me, and I'd like to say I'd always been there for her, but I'm not sure of anything anymore. The things she'd told me about my friends—how they'd been cruel to her and I'd never known it—it makes me angry, and it makes me wonder how good a friend I'd really been. She was always my best friend, but was I always hers?

Chapter Thirty-One

Casey

"Oh, that feels so good, Case," he groaned as I ground my lower body against his.

"Mmm," I moaned in agreement, leaving open-mouthed kisses on his neck. I could have gotten off just like this, but I wanted more. No, I needed more.

"Damn, baby." Decker's hands moved from my thighs, which were straddling his waist, to my ass and he squeezed, pressing me harder against him.

Good. That meant I was getting to him as much as he was getting to me. It had been the same song and dance since we shared our first kiss a few months ago. We couldn't seem

*to keep our hands off each other. Each night,
after our parents went to bed, Decker would
sneak in my bedroom window, and we'd make
out, fondle, rub, and stroke. We'd rounded all
the bases except for that elusive home run.*

*But tonight I was hoping to change that. My
parents and his parents were both out for their
weekly date night. This time, it was out of
town. Tonight, we were alone. All. Night. Long.*

*I slowed my movements and looked into his
green eyes, now dark with desire. "I'm ready,
Deck."*

*His eyes widened for a fraction of a second
before he closed them tightly and shook his
head. "No, Case. Anything but that."*

*I growled in frustration and sat up so my
upper body was at a right angle to his. "What
is the problem, Decker? Are you not attracted
to me like that?" I glared down at him.*

*He rolled his eyes and held on to my hips,
then raised his core to meet mine, causing me
to groan. "Does it feel like I'm not attracted to
you?"*

*"Then what's the problem?" I knew I was
whining, but I didn't care. "What are we
waiting for?"*

*He sighed. "You deserve something special,
Casey. Roses and candles and all that
romantic shit."*

*Now it was my turn to roll my eyes. "I don't
care about all that stuff, Decker. If it's with*

you, it will be special. I don't need all that superficial stuff. I just need you."

And that was true. I experienced all my intimate firsts with Decker, and none of them had been accompanied by candlelight or flowers. It was always just me and Decker, and that alone had made those moments amazing.

"Casey—"

He started to argue, but I silenced him by taking off my shirt. I wasn't wearing a bra. Decker was a boob man and the mere sight of my breasts turned him into putty in my hands. Sure, it was an underhanded move, but I was much more likely to get my way when I was topless.

"Please, Decker," I begged as I grabbed his hands and placed one on each breast, grinding against him, long and slow. Yeah, I was probably going to hell for trying to seduce the virginity out of him. "I need you so bad," I added for good measure.

Decker groaned, and in one swift move he flipped us over so he was on top. "You're an evil little person," he whispered in my ear as he trailed a line of kisses down the side of my neck, along my collarbone, and down to my breasts.

I moaned as he took a nipple into his mouth, squeezing the other one between his thumb and forefinger. My hips thrust up towards his.

"Uh-uh," he said. "If we're doing this, we do it my way."

I sighed in frustration. "Don't tease me, Decker."

He looked up at me and smirked. "I'm going to make you feel so good, Casey."

Beep.

He moved further down my body. Kissing his way past my ribs and circling my navel.

Beep.

He bit down slightly near my hip bone, causing me to squirm.

Beep beep.

He hooked his fingers over the waistband of my shorts and slowly pulled them down.

"Don't stop, Decker. Please."

"Never, baby."

Beep. Beep beep.

"I think she's starting to wake up," a distant voice says.

Beep.

What the hell is that beeping? And who is that speaking?

I fight to open my eyes through the thick haze filling my head. I'd been dreaming of my first time with Decker, and I really don't like that I'd been interrupted. It'd felt so real.

I open my right eye slightly, squinting to take in the scene around me. White walls. Blue curtain. Drop ceiling. Hell with fluorescent lighting. Yay, I'm in the hospital. I close my eye and will it all to go away.

"Casey?" a familiar voice says. It's Kate. I feel her put her hand in mine. "If you can hear me, squeeze my hand." I squeeze. "She's responsive," she tells someone.

"I'll go get the doctor," the other person—a guy, I think—says.

"You scared the hell out of me, Casey Evans," Kate scolds once the door clicks behind the mystery person.

"Sorry," I think I say; I try to at least.

"Sorry isn't going to cut it," she says angrily. I hate it when she rags on me about this. I wish I could open my damn eyes, but I feel so sleepy.

"What happened?" I'm not entirely sure I'm speaking clearly, or at all, but she answers me so I guess she understands.

"You had a cardiac episode."

I wince. That hasn't happened in a while.

"You nearly arrested in the ambulance on the way to the hospital."

I winced again. "Decker?"

Kate laughs, not in humor but disgust. Disgust at me for keeping this from him. "You're just lucky he wasn't around."

"I kicked him out," I say quietly. Almost hoping that she doesn't hear me. Almost.

"You what?"

I struggle to open my eyes again and manage a slight squint. I look over at Kate. She's standing at my bedside, wide-eyed and looking completely disheveled.

I did this to her. Again.

"I'm sorry," I tell her.

"For what, exactly? For almost dying in our apartment? Not for the first time, I might add. For scaring the shit out of me? Again, not for the first time." She's ticking each item off on her fingers. "For not telling the guy you are *so* obviously in love with that you have a heart condition that you refuse to seek help for? Which one is it, Casey? What exactly are you sorry for?"

I close my eyes again, not able to take the fear and anger plastered on Kate's face. I'm a coward. "For everything," I tell her. "All of that. I'm sorry for all of it."

She takes my hand again. "I love you, Casey. You know that. You're my best friend. I've stood by you through so much, and you've stood by me, too. But I can't do this anymore. I can't watch you self-destruct. Coming home this afternoon and not being able to wake you up? You were starting to turn *blue*. I thought it was the end. The *end* end. I was so scared."

I open my eyes again, a little wider this time. Kate has tears streaming down both her cheeks. My heart breaks, more than it's already broken, at the sight before me. My quiet but otherwise completely strong roommate is breaking, and it's my fault.

"I'm sorry, Kate."

"Sorry isn't good enough, Casey!"

I cringe at her volume, but I know I deserve everything she throws at me. "Then what *do* you want me to say?"

"Nothing! I don't want you to *say* anything. I want you to *do*!"

"Well, that's not going to happen," I say quietly.

Kate shakes her head. "I can't sit by and watch you kill yourself any longer."

I roll my eyes. "That's a bit dramatic, don't you think?"

"No, I don't think it is."

"I'm not killing myself, Kate. My body is doing a damn good job of that on its own."

"You're refusing treatment," she spits, crossing her arms over her chest.

"I take my medication," I argue.

"You're prolonging your life, Casey. You're not saving it."

"It's my decision to make!" The machine beside me is beeping more urgently, and Kate takes a step back, trying to regroup.

"You're right, Casey. It is your decision. And it's my decision not to be a part of it anymore." Big tears spill out of her eyes and rapidly fall down her cheeks.

"What are you saying?" My voice is quiet, childlike. Kate has been my rock throughout all this. Ever since I'd been diagnosed two years ago, it's been her and me. She's the only reason my parents had felt it was okay to leave me here in California and hadn't forced me to go home. Because Kate is here. She's solid. She's my person.

"I'm saying I can't sit back and wait with you for you to die anymore. I understand that I don't know what's it's like to be you, to be diagnosed with a potentially terminal disease. But Casey, you have options. This doesn't have to be a dead end street for you. There are roads where you can turn off and you won't explore them...you won't even slow the car down. You're twenty-one years old, and you've given up on yourself."

"Kate, we've talked about this–"

"No, we haven't talked about this. The doctor laid it all out for you and you chose. And you chose poorly. I don't know what made you give up on life, Casey. But I can't handle it anymore. I may be strong, but I'm not that strong. I can't watch my best friend fall apart this way when there is a solution. The Casey I met freshman year was a fighter. Where did she go?"

Silent tears stream down my face because she's right. I had been a fighter. I used to be strong. I'd left my hometown all by myself and forged a life for myself in California. I had dreams and goals, and I let this disease take them away. I should be ashamed of myself, but instead I'm just numb. Weak.

The door opens, and Jay walks in, in all his tattooed glory. He looks between Kate and me, forehead crinkling at the sight of our tears. "The doctor will be here in a minute."

Kate nods and gives him a small smile. She steps back up to the side of my bed, leans forward and kisses the crown of my head. "I love you, Casey. Please," her voice cracks, and she takes a moment to regroup, "please take care of yourself."

I close my eyes, afraid that if I keep them open and watch Kate walk out that door, I'll break. I feel the hot tears trail down, and I can taste their saltiness on my lips. I feel like I'm drowning in them. Once I hear the click of the door shutting, the first sob breaks free. Then the second.

My best friend just walked out on me, and I can't even blame her for it. And if my other best friend knew what I'd been keeping from him, he'd probably walk out, too.

The worst part...I totally deserve it.

Chapter Thirty-Two

Decker

I feel a small thump on my shoulder.

"Decker?"

Another thump, this one heavier.

"Decker!"

I slowly open my eyes and see Kate peering down at me. Jay's beside her, looking as serious as ever.

"Why does this keep happening?" I ask as I rub the sleep from my eyes, referring to the fact that this is the second time I've been woken up on the floor outside of Casey's apartment. Kate doesn't respond, so I look up to her and note the sadness I missed before.

I quickly rise to my feet, my insides filling with dread. "Is it Casey?"

Kate's knees buckle beneath her, and Jay quickly grabs hold of her so she doesn't fall. Sobs burst from her chest, and Jay pulls her close, tucking her head under his chin.

I can't breathe.

"Why don't we go inside?" Jay suggests, nodding to the door.

I pull out the spare key I swiped days before and unlock the door, pushing it open and stepping aside so Jay can walk Kate through. He takes her over to the couch, where she collapses in a heap of tears and sniffles.

I stiffly make my way across the room and sit down on the armchair caddy corner to the couch. Casey's not here. Kate's hysterical. Jay's not talking, which is a surprise since he was so chatty at the club last night. I desperately want to know what the hell is going on, but I can't find the words.

Jay appears with a glass of water and sits down beside Kate, pulling her into his side. After a few minutes she calms down enough to take a drink. Then she starts talking.

"Casey's at the hospital," she says, and I immediately jump to my feet. "Wait," Kate says. "There are things you need to know."

I look between Kate and the door, badly wanting to follow my instincts and rush off to be by Casey's side. To be there for her. But the pleading look on Kate's tearstained face convinces me to hear her out. I nod and sit back down.

Kate lets out a deep breath and continues. "Casey has a heart problem."

My eyes widen, and my fingers dig into my jean-clad thighs. *No...not my Casey.*

"She was diagnosed about two and a half years ago, during freshman year. They don't know when the problem started exactly...how long she's had it. But she's been managing it pretty well with medication and a healthy lifestyle. But," she pauses to collect herself, "her heart is very weak." Her voice breaks at the end, and I see Jay squeeze her hand.

All I can think about right at this moment is who was holding Casey's hand when she received this diagnosis? Was she alone? Was she scared? *Of course she was scared, you idiot.* But is she still scared? Who is with her now? Is she alone? Is someone holding her hand? Why hadn't she told me? I knew Casey was hiding something all this time, but I never would have guessed it was something so...life altering.

"Is she okay right now?" I finally ask.

Kate looks down and sniffles, before looking up and meeting my eyes. "She's stable."

I let out a breath I didn't realize I'd been holding. "Thank God."

"Decker," she says firmly, getting my attention. "Like I said, her heart is very weak. It can't handle much more trauma, and today she had a cardiac episode. She passed out and stopped breathing. I had to give her CPR when I got home; she was turning blue from lack of oxygen. I don't know how long she was out, but fortunately she woke up while I was at the hospital."

I take my head in my hands. CPR? Lack of oxygen? That means she could have died. If Kate hadn't gotten home when she did, Casey could have died. I fist my hair in my hands. It's my fault. It's all my fault. If I hadn't upset her earlier, maybe this wouldn't have happened. *Shit!* Was I still outside her door while she was inside almost dying?

I get up and start pacing the room. My hands are still in my hair, and I want to pull every last one out.

"Decker, I'm so sorry to be the one to tell you all this. Casey should have told you. I told her to tell you."

I stop pacing and look at Kate. "What else?"

Kate's wringing her hands in her lap. I can see the internal debate through her eyes, she's trying to decide how much to tell me. I'll make is easy on her.

"Tell me everything. Please?"

She looks to Jay, for support I guess, and he nods. It makes me want to hug him. And at the same time, it makes me want to punch him because he obviously knows more about my Casey than I do and that pisses me off. Though I'm sure it's Kate who told him and not Casey.

"Like I said, she's stable now. But she almost arrested in the ambulance on the way to the hospital. It's likely due to all the stress she's been under since her dad died, driving cross-country twice, and just running herself ragged. She gets into these spells where she doesn't take the best care of herself, and usually I'm able to straighten her out before anything happens, but I think all the added stress put a greater strain on her."

Added stress. A.K.A. me. I'm the added stress. No wonder she kept trying to leave me behind. She was trying to save her own life. With that realization, I slump back onto the chair, causing it to scrape against the hardwood floor as it slides backwards.

"It's me, isn't it?" I vocalize my worst fear. "It's my fault. I should have stayed away when she asked me to."

"No! Oh, God no, Decker." Kate rushes off the couch and kneels in front of me, grabbing my hands in hers. "It is *not* your fault. Casey's heart has been this way for years. Nothing you did caused this."

"But I wasn't here, and she was fine. Now I'm here, and she's not." My voice is flat, emotionless. "We fought today, Kate. Did she tell you that? I found her pills. I asked her about it, and she freaked out. I made her upset."

Kate shakes her head. "No, Decker. It's not your fault," she says quietly. "Casey hasn't been 'fine' for a long time. This was inevitable."

"Why did this have to happen to her? She's so good. She's always been a good girl. She is a straight A student. She never breaks the rules. Why did this happen to her?" I finally lose my composure and break. A sound like I've never heard before comes from my chest as I collapse on myself. I can feel Kate's arms around me and hear her make soothing sounds that are probably words but I can't make them out. All I can think about is my best friend. I might lose my best friend.

Forever.

Chapter Thirty-Three

Casey

When I wake from crying myself to sleep, it's dark outside, and I see the silhouette of my mom in the chair beside the hospital bed. She sits up and takes my hand once she sees my eyes open.

"Hi, Mom." My voice is scratchy. She immediately goes into mom-mode, pouring me a paper cup of water from the pink pitcher on the bedside table. I thank her when she hands it to me and take a long sip.

"Casey," she says on a sigh.

I set the cup down on the table and lean back, knowing she's about to light into me about how important it is to take care of myself. Surprisingly, she doesn't. She does something even worse. She cries. She leans forward so her forehead is resting on the white hospital sheet, and she cries.

"Mom?" I ask, running my hand over her head, through her hair, because I'm unsure of what else to do. My mom has always been the strong one when I've been in the hospital. The rock. I'm not sure I can show her that same strength in return.

I watch as she tries to pull herself together, looking everywhere but at me. A horrible feeling moves through me, taking over my entire body. One that hasn't made an appearance since the early days of my diagnosis. Fear.

"Tell me," I say in a small voice.

She takes a deep breath and holds my hand. "I spoke with Dr. Andrews regarding your test results. She wants to discuss everything with Dr. Smythe, but the preliminary blood test results indicate an infection."

"Endocarditis?" I ask, referring to an infection people with heart problems are susceptible to.

"They'll need to perform more tests to be sure, but it's likely."

I sigh in relief. Well, that's not the end of my world. A healthy dose of antibiotics can beat that out of me. Mom knows this, so I'm not sure why she's still looking so somber.

"Is there something else?"

Her eyes well up with tears, and I try to swallow the lump that's formed in my throat.

"The ECG indicated an irregular heartbeat."

"That's not uncommon," I remind her.

"They did a chest x-ray while you were asleep."

I sigh. No use in beating around the bush. "So it's bad."

"The infection seems to have affected your valves, caused your heart to become more enlarged. They want to do more scans to see the severity of the damage. Dr. Andrews didn't say much—she didn't want to without speaking with Dr. Smythe first—but I could just tell, Casey." The tears she'd been holding back fell.

"Mom, calm down. Let's just wait and see what Dr. Smythe has to say. He knows my heart better than Dr. Andrews does. He's been my cardiologist for over two years. Plus, I feel fine. I don't feel any different."

"Damn it, Casey." I startle at her angry tone. "Don't you understand? Your condition is terminal. One day, the news *isn't* going to be good. This might be that day."

"You don't think I know that?" I yell at her as she stands up and turns towards the window.

"I just feel like you've been living the last couple years in denial, Casey. You're barely acknowledging the situation. You're barely living. You're twenty-one years old, so young, and yet you're ready to just let this disease take you from me. I just lost your father; I don't want to lose my daughter, too."

And I think my mom has finally reached her tipping point.

Before my dad died, my mom had him to lean on when I was sick and would have had him when I died, too. But now he's gone. Her husband is gone, and her daughter is dying. She has no one. No one but me.

And I won't be around much longer.

"Casey," she says in a resigned tone, still looking out the window. "I know you're firm in your decision on how you want to live out the rest of your life. As much as I have always hated it, I have respected it because you probably feel as though it's the only thing you actually have control over, but I prayed like crazy you'd change your mind. But right now I'm going to be selfish because this is all becoming way too real." She turns from the window, and I look up from studying my hands to meet her eyes, eyes that are a perfect match to my own. "Please reconsider."

I start to shake my head, but she starts speaking again, interrupting what I am about to say.

"I saw you when you were back home with Decker. You were happy. You were *you* again. Kate said you've been different since you've been back here, too. I just think that maybe you need to reevaluate your decision. Things are different now from how they were before. Decker is–"

"Don't bring him into this," I warn.

She shakes her head. "You get your stubbornness from your father, did you know that?"

"Yeah," I scowl, not wanting to talk about my dad but knowing that it's coming regardless.

"A few days before his heart attack he was complaining of chest pains. I tried to get him to go see a doctor, but of course he wouldn't go. Next thing we knew he was in the hospital, and the first thing he said to me was that he should have seen the doctor when he had the chance. Casey, you have that chance. Don't let it pass you by."

"It's not that easy," I say, swallowing down the ever-present lump in my throat.

My mom sits back down and holds my hand again as I start to cry. "Then talk to me, Casey. Let me help you."

"I'm scared, Mom."

She smiles a sad smile. "I know you are, baby. I'm scared, too. But know that if you do this, I will be with you every step of the way. You will not be alone. And I have faith that you are going to be just fine."

"But what if it doesn't work? What if my body rejects it? Or I die during surgery?"

"Casey, if you don't have the surgery, you'll die anyway." Apparently we're going for the blunt approach today. My mom and Kate must have attended the same shock and awe training. "The question is, would you rather die fighting...or giving up?"

If I go down, how do I want it to be? As a coward or a warrior?

"I need time. I need to think." I don't really plan to think about it. I know I'm being selfish, but the truth is I'm completely terrified and avoidance is my go-to defense mechanism.

"That's all I ask. We can see what Dr. Smythe has to say, too." She smiles and pushes a loose strand of my hair behind my ear. "I love you."

"I love you, too, Mom." She stands up, and I hold on tighter to her hand. "Where are you going?" I'm not ready for her to leave me. I don't want to be alone. How ironic, considering I've spent the better part of three years pushing everyone away.

"I'm going to head down to the cafeteria and grab something to eat. I'll be right back."

I let go of her hand, knowing she's probably starving and exhausted from the impromptu trip across the country. I hadn't even thought about how she got here. My guess is that Kate had called her right away.

"I'd offer to get you something–"

"But I can't eat anything but sawdust while I'm in the joint. I got it."

She laughs at my cynicism. "I'll see if I can sneak in something since you slept through dinner."

"You rebel." I watch her walk from the room, quietly shutting the door behind her, then lay my head back and sigh.

What the hell do I do?

Chapter Thirty-Four

Decker

Room 201.

You'd think that would be the first room when you step off the elevator at the end of the hall. But it's not. It's not the last room either. How do I know this? Because I've been up and down the hall twice. Room 201 is not here. That number does not exist in this damn hospital's numbering system.

200.

The next door is 202.

Two down is labeled 208.

Four more is 218. It doesn't even make sense.

Who the hell numbered this place?

Taking a break from pacing the floor, I lean up against the wall and rub my face with my hands, when a soft voice asks "Sir, can I help you find your way?"

If you only knew how convoluted that question actually is.

"I'm looking for room 201. Casey Evans."

"201 is in the cardiac wing," the young nurse tells me.

"That makes sense, but I have no idea where that is," I tell her, pushing myself off the wall, eager to follow whatever directions she's going to give me.

"All the odd numbers on this floor are cardiac. It can be confusing if you don't know," she says with an understanding smile. "Follow me."

"Thank you," I say as I fall in step behind her.

"Visiting family?" she asks.

"No, a friend. My best friend."

A flash of sadness crosses over her face, then she gives a sympathetic nod. "I'm sorry your friend is in the hospital." The way she says it makes me believe she actually means it. You'd think working in a hospital dealing with illness all the time would numb you to it, but this nurse seems truly compassionate.

"Thank you."

She leads me through a set of double doors I had ignored during my laps. They're locked, but fortunately she has the little magnetic card that deactivates the locking mechanism. She gives a small smile to the burly male orderly working the security desk as we walk by.

Looking at the watch on her wrist, she tells me "Visiting hours are over in about twenty minutes. Looks like you got here just in time. I'm sorry you don't have more time though."

My stomach rolls at her statement. I know she didn't mean it the way I'm thinking, but the mere thought that my time with Casey in general may be limited makes me sick.

I can't lose her.

As we near the end of the hall, the nurse points to a small alcove elevator bank. "You can take those down when you leave. You can even take them up when you come back. Just remember the C elevators."

"C for cardiac." *C for Casey.* "Shouldn't be that hard."

She smiles as me and gestures to the last door on the right. "There it is. I wish your friend well."

I reach my hand out to shake hers. "Thank you…"

"Laura," she supplies, shaking my hand.

"Thank you, Laura. I'm Decker, and I'd probably be wandering the halls until way past visiting hours had you not shown up."

"It's my pleasure. Take care, Decker." She turns around and walks back the way we came. I watch her go, not yet ready to face what's behind door 201. But the sound of a door opening behind me finally makes me turn around.

It's Casey's mom. She quietly steps out of the room, not yet noticing me, and shuts the door behind her. In this moment, she and Casey could be twins, they look so much alike. She's looking down, clutching her hand to her chest. Once the door is completely closed, she leans back against the wall and slides down to the floor. I can tell by the way her shoulders are shaking that she's crying.

I panic.

This can't be good!

I rush over and fall to my knees in front of her. "Mrs. Evans?"

She lifts her head from where it was resting on her knees, and all I can see is sadness and utter devastation in the tear soaked brown depths that are identical to her daughter's. When she recognizes me, she smiles through her sobs and grips my arms.

~ 270 ~

Her fingers are digging into my forearms, but I feel no pain, only numbness.

"Decker, you have to talk to her. You have to make her realize she's making a mistake."

"Casey's okay?" I ask, ignoring her request. If she wants me to talk to her, then she's got to be okay.

More tears spill from her eyes as she shakes her head. I instantly feel pain everywhere. No. Casey's not okay.

"She's got an infection. Her cardiologist hasn't been by yet, just an attending physician, so we don't know the specifics. But it's not good, Decker. You've got to talk to her. She's been different since she's been with you again. It's like she's been living again. You make her feel alive. You may be the one to get through to her."

"Get through to her how?" I ask, shaking my head. "I'm not sure I understand."

"She needs a transplant. A heart transplant."

A heart transplant. My Casey needs a new heart.

My immediate thought is that she can have mine! Because I sure as hell don't want it if she's not going to be around for me to love.

My stomach rolls again.

A new heart? Her *heart* needs to be *replaced*? It's *that* broken that it's not working properly? It may even be hurting her. It *is* hurting her; otherwise, she wouldn't need a transplant. Her heart. It's what she loves me with. I know she loves me, even if she won't say it.

"Isn't there a list or something?" I mumble, thinking back to all the TV shows and movies I've ever seen with transplants. She made me watch so much *Grey's Anatomy*, I should know this! "Is she on the list?"

Mrs. Evans's shoulders sink further, if that's even possible. "She doesn't want the transplant. She could have been put on the list two years ago, but she said no."

She said no?

"What?"

"She's afraid, Decker. She's scared of dying."

"But a new heart would help her?" I say more as a question than as a statement. I'm so confused. "If she's afraid of dying, why wouldn't she get the transplant?"

"A transplant can help her. The downside to transplants is that her body could reject the heart. And of course there are the usual risks, as with any surgery."

I don't want to hear that.

"So she could die either way," I say, resigned. I could lose Casey either way.

Her mom frowns but nods.

That's the ugliest truth I've ever been exposed to. Casey could die whether she gets the transplant or not. There may be no saving the girl I've loved almost my entire life.

Just when I got her back...

"I'll talk to her," I tell Mrs. Evans. "But visiting hours are about done for the night."

Mrs. Evans's eyes brighten up, and she finally releases my forearms. I swear I'm going to have nail marks in my arms. She slides her hands down to mine and gently squeezes them. "You're family, Decker. Visiting hours don't apply to family."

"Is that hospital policy?" I ask with a small smile. It's about all I can manage, and even it feels forced.

"Policy shmolicy," Mrs. Evans says as she releases my hands and starts to push herself up off the floor. I rise to my feet first and pull her up. She looks up at me once we're standing. "Thank you, Decker. I'm...I'm sorry we didn't tell you about her condition. I'm sorry we kept it from you. I always thought you deserved to know everything, but Casey was adamant and we, her father and I, were too afraid to upset her."

"It's okay," I tell her, even though it's not. It's not okay I didn't know my best friend had been given a death sentence.

I'm hurt the Evans hadn't told me, but I can sort of understand where they were coming from. Casey had to be their number one priority, and they hadn't wanted to upset her. I'm hurt my parents most likely knew and didn't tell me either. I'm their son. If they knew, they should have told me so I could have been there for Casey.

But most of all...I'm hurt Casey hadn't told me. Regardless of our falling out—whatever it was—this is so much bigger than that. So much bigger than that. She should have told me.

"I'll talk to her," I promise.

Mrs. Evans wraps her arms around me in one of those amazing mom hugs that almost make everything better again. *Almost.* "Thank you, Decker." She takes a step back. "I'm going to head down to the cafeteria to get something to eat. I'll bring you back a snack."

I start to tell her she doesn't have to, but she gives me a mom look and the argument dies in my throat. "Thanks, that'll be great."

"Go on in, she just woke up a little while ago. She probably won't be falling back asleep any time soon. She's been out most of the day." She nudges me towards the door once she realizes I'm not moving.

Bracing myself for what may be the scariest moment of my life, I reach for the handle on the door and push.

Chapter Thirty-Five

Casey

The fancy remote that controls the reclining feature of the hospital bed is something I am all too familiar with. I use it to raise myself to a seated position and make note of the time on the wall clock. It's almost nine. Visiting hours are almost over, I know them by heart by now. By heart—ha-ha—no pun intended.

I'm a little disappointed Decker didn't come by today. I know, what right do I have to even think that after the way I treated him today? I can't believe I threw him out of the apartment. Especially after the amazing time we'd spent together last night. Things had changed between us—again—last night. We had the chance to do it right this time.

But I'd gone and screwed it all up.

I'd been mentally raw. Being with him like that again...it brought back all those feelings I'd tried to bury deep within my heart. They'd been right there on the surface, exposed, and when everything had erupted—when I'd erupted—it was a vivid explosion of emotion.

It was a mess. *I* was a mess. Hell, I'm still a mess.

And poor Decker. He'd had to bear the brunt of it.

What else was new, right?

I shouldn't have freaked out on him the way that I did. I know that now. I panicked. I just didn't want him to ever find out about my broken heart...my ill fate. I'd wanted him to continue to live his life pure and happy...to forget me. I still want that for him.

But after last night...it's clear that would never happen. At least it had been clear.

I think I really messed things up this time. Maybe it was for the best.

I hear the door open and call out to my mom. "You're back quick. Kitchen closed?"

There's a light blue curtain hanging beside my bed, blocking my view of the door, so I can't see what she's doing. I hear the shuffle of feet, so I know someone has entered the room.

"Mom?"

I hear a familiar sigh—one that makes my heart race. I know this because the beeps on the heart monitor have increased their pace. Which means he knows it, too. *How embarrassing.* Decker steps around the curtain, and when our eyes meet, my heart skips a beat. Yep, monitor gave that one away, too. *Traitor.*

The confusion, hurt, and utter sadness on his face cause me to drop my gaze.

This is what I hadn't wanted—to cause him pain.

I feel the burn of unwanted tears behind my eyes and use what little willpower I have left to keep them at bay, distracting myself by picking at a loose thread on the sterile white blanket.

"Hey," he says solemnly.

I startle as I feel the bed dip; I hadn't realized he'd gotten so close.

"Hey," I don't look up. I just can't.

There are several minutes of near silence. The only sounds are those coming from the assortment of machines surrounding the bed.

"So...what do we have to do to bust you out of here?" Decker asks. My eyes shoot up to his, trying to gage the seriousness of his question. The slight smile on his sad face tells me everything I need to know—everything that's important.

He forgives me.

This beautiful man—who I've emotionally beaten down, repeatedly—forgives me. What did I ever do to deserve him in my life?

I offer him a small smile in return and promptly burst into tears. Somehow, he manages to lie down beside me on the narrow bed and pulls me into his muscular chest, rubbing my back in soothing circles.

"I'm so sorry, Decker. I'm sorry I hurt you. I'm sorry I keep hurting you." I don't know if he can hear me through my sobs, but I know he knows.

After an exceptionally long-awaited cry on my best friend's shoulder, I settle down, readying myself for the barrage of questions I know he's going to have. And he deserves answers, lord does he deserve answers.

I take a deep breath and ask the one thing that's on the tip of my tongue. I know the answer, but I need to hear him say it. Even though I may not deserve his response.

"Do you hate me?"

He pulls away from me, and I frown at the loss of contact. Using his thumb and forefinger, he lifts my chin so I'm looking in his eyes. "I could *never* hate you, Casey.

Never. I may be angry with you, but my love for you will always be more than that. Always."

Two big tears escape my eyes, and Decker cradles my face in his hands, using his thumbs to dry my cheeks.

"Think we can stop making mistakes now?"

I nod in response and sniffle, tucking myself back into his chest.

"You know you're going to need to talk to me, right?" He runs his fingers through my hair, occasionally getting stuck in a hospital-induced knot. I swear they're a thing.

I nod again.

"And you're going to need to use your words?"

"Yes," I whisper.

"In a voice something other than a dog can hear?"

"But you heard me, does that make you a dog?"

He laughs. "Yeah, I guess it does. As long as you'll always be my bitch."

I pull back, a look of shock on my face as I swat his arm. "I can't believe you called me a bitch!"

He raises an eyebrow at me. "All things considered, Case?"

"You have a point," I concede, resting my head back down. He smells so good. So Decker-ish. I wish I could bottle his scent and keep it forever. The thought of forever brings me back to reality, and I nestle in closer.

"Tell me everything," he says quietly. And I can hear it in his voice—he's begging me to let him in. Once and for all.

And I will.

It's time. It's long past time.

"How much do you already know?" I ask, certain he's already spoken with Kate and my mother but uncertain as to what they'd told him. I mean he's here, so someone had to tell him what was up. I'm in the cardiac wing, for crying out loud. It's not like he thinks I'm here for a sore throat or sprained ankle.

"It doesn't matter. I want to hear it from you."

Chapter Thirty-Six

Decker

It's crazy how machines can so effectively measure your life. Take the heart monitor Casey's connected to for instance. When I'd arrived earlier, it sped up when Casey became aware of who was here. I made her heart race. Now, it's picking up speed again, and I know it's because she's nervous. I can feel the tension in her body. I rub her back, trying to ease some of the tautness.

"Why don't you just start at the beginning?" I offer.

I can feel her chest expand as she takes a deep breath in, and her warm breath hits my chest on its way out. She repeats those movements one more time before she starts speaking.

"My freshman year, just before Thanksgiving, I went into cardiac arrest." My breath catches, and she pauses for a moment; I give her a squeeze to continue. "Fortunately Kate was with in our dorm and did CPR until the ambulance got there, which luckily didn't take long either. My memories of that day are a little fuzzy. I remember not feeling well before, but I chalked it up to being stressed out. College is a lot different from high school, ya know?" I nod in response, though I know it was a rhetorical question.

"Anyway, I'd been feeling tired, a little lightheaded, nauseated, and just overall fatigued. But I was studying real hard and taking a bunch of classes, so I didn't think anything of it. I never had chest pains or anything like that. When it happened, it was sudden; I don't remember anything other than studying with Kate and then waking up in the hospital. They told me my heart actually stopped."

She whispers that last part, and I stop my ministrations and pull her closer to me. *Her heart stopped.* If she'd been alone, she'd have been gone. My Casey would have been gone forever and my last moments with her would have been selfish, drunken ones. I can't even imagine what getting that phone call would have been like. I'm so thankful I don't have to.

Holy shit.

"I know, right?"

I must have said that last part out loud.

"I can't even imagine what that must have been like," I say honestly. My shoulder injury and all the end-of-the-world drama I'd created for myself when I'd learned I couldn't play baseball anymore was *nothing* compared to what Casey went through. My shoulder stopped working...well, her heart stopped working. Really puts things into perspective.

"It was horrifying. I was so scared when I woke up and didn't know where I was. My mom and dad hadn't arrived yet, and they wouldn't let Kate back to see me because she wasn't family. All I had was a nurse with a horrible bedside manner who kept saying 'the doctor will be in to see you shortly' every time I asked a question."

"I wish I could have been there for you." I place a kiss on the top of her head. Her hair smells sterile, hospital-like. I don't like it.

"I wished for you a lot of times," she murmurs into my chest. "But I just couldn't bear to bring you into the clusterfuck that had become my life. I couldn't suck you into it, because I knew you'd never get out. One of us had to survive, you know? Has to survive..."

I push back from her and lift her chin so she's looking at me. "Let's get one thing

~ 284 ~

straight, okay?" I wait for her to nod and when she does I continue. "There's nothing we can do to change the past, we'll never forget it but we can't dwell on it. So we're moving forward now, and you're going to deal with the fact that I'm here. I'm in your life once and for all. And you're going to stop trying to push me out of it. Got it?"

Casey blinks back a few tears and nods. "I got it."

"Good." I lean in and kiss her forehead, her cheeks, the tip of her nose, and finally her lips. She's a little salty from her tears, mixed with a little sweet that's all her.

She smiles slightly against my lips, but pulls away. "There's more, Decker. Lots more."

"Tell me."

"This is really hard," she sniffles and burrows deeper.

"I know, baby. But I'm right here, and I'm not going anywhere."

It's obviously difficult for her to talk about, for good reason, and I almost feel like an asshole for pushing her, but she can't keep it from me any longer. If we're going to move forward—together—then everything needs to be out on the table. I need to know it all. Deep down, I know she knows that, although I'm not so sure about the moving forward part since, according to her mom, she doesn't want the transplant that will save her life. The thought pains me.

I decide to try to help her along. "Kate mentioned that you had a heart problem. What exactly does that mean? There are a lot of different heart problems on the web. She said the doctors don't really know when it started?"

She sighs and pulls her head back a bit so she can speak. "It means I could have been born with it, or it could have developed later on. I never showed any symptoms prior to that first hospitalization, so the doctors' couldn't say anything definite."

"Why now though? Why did it suddenly start hurting you? Did something bring it on?" I don't understand. Why couldn't she have lived her whole life without this affecting her?

I feel her body tense up, a small sign that there is more bad news to come. Though I'm not sure how that can even be possible. Nothing could be worse than what she's already told me.

"Deck, I'm really scared to tell you this part," she confesses.

"Casey, baby, you can tell me anything." And she can. Always.

"I just...I don't want you to think any less of me for it."

I remove my hands from around her and place them on her cheeks, moving her face so she's looking at me. Brushing the tip of my nose against hers, I tell her "Nothing, absolutely nothing, will make me think less of you. I promise." I punctuate that statement with a soft kiss on her lips.

Her eyes are glossy, and she breaks eye contact before she speaks.

"I was pregnant."

I'm stunned silent. *Casey—my Casey—was pregnant?* And she thought I'd think less of her for it? I feel hot tension throughout my body as I think about beating the shit out of the guy who got her pregnant and obviously bailed—since she'd been alone that day in the hospital and is still unattached. What a douche. But think less of her? Never.

"Casey, I'd never think less of you for that. I'm sorry." I place gentle kisses on her forehead, attempting to loosen her up since her body is still rigid. "I'm sorry for everything that you've gone through. And I'm sorry that the jerk who got you pregnant wasn't there for you." I look into her eyes and see the tears flowing. I wipe them with my thumbs, while gently cupping her face.

"I didn't know," she quickly adds. "Honestly, I was so busy with school that I barely paid attention to my period, and when I noticed it was late, I chalked it up to stress. I never would have guessed I was pregnant."

"I'm sorry, baby. But I still don't have to like the guy."

"I never told him," she whispers, almost as though she's talking to herself. "He didn't know." Her body shudders, and I hold her tight. Jeez, my girl holds the weight of the world on her shoulders. And I have no idea how to make it better.

"It's okay," I tell her, continuing to softly rub her back.

"It's not okay!" she cries out, pushing me away. I stumble back, almost falling off the small bed. Thank God for the short rail on the upper portion of the bed. Shocked, I stand up and take a step back since she clearly needs a little space.

"Look, Case, I don't want you getting upset." I gesture to the heart monitor that is beeping a bit faster now. "We can talk more tomorrow. Visiting hours are over anyway." I give her a smile, attempting to convey that I am not brushing her off after her big confession, but rather I'm concerned for her health, which is the whole truth.

She's lying on her back now, blankly looking up at the ceiling, tears streaming down her cheeks. So sad. So broken. I want to climb back into that too-small bed with her and hold her all night long. But she's exhausted and needs her rest. I step back to her bedside and lean in to kiss her head.

"I've only ever been with you, Decker," she says when my lips touch her skin. Her voice so quiet, I wouldn't have heard her if I hadn't been learning in.

I still, my mind trying to comprehend the importance of that statement while, at the same time, fiercely combatting it away.

I've only ever been with you.

I was pregnant.

Was.

Only.

Ever.

You.

I pull back and look at her. "Me?"

She closes her eyes and nods. "Yes."

Chapter Thirty-Seven

Casey

I watch as Decker raises his tight fist up to his open mouth and bites down. His eyes are a picture of tortured devastation, and his knuckles are white. I did that. My secrets did that. My selfishness broke this beautiful man standing before me. He turns away from me, raking his free hand through his hair.

I sob, knowing that this is it. This is when Decker finally decides he's had enough of me and my shit. I roll to my side, away from him, and curl up into myself, not able to stomach watching him walk away. The sobs wrack through me, causing me to lose my breath and the machines to make noise.

Saying goodbye to everything I'd ever known and moving across the country hadn't broken me. Losing a baby I hadn't known I'd had inside me and being diagnosed with a death sentence on the same day hadn't broken me either. But this right here—knowing that Decker is going to leave me and never come back—is making my life flash before my eyes.

I see us meeting as six-year-olds...smiling the cheesiest smiles as elementary school graduates...awkwardly slow dancing at our eighth grade dance...me cheering him on at his baseball games...our first kiss...our first time...hugging at high school graduation...being back together again...

"Shh..." I feel him settle behind me, the dip of the thin mattress, his body curved tightly against mine, arms wrapped tightly around me while still mindful of the wires attached to me. "Shh, it's okay, baby. I'm right here. I'm not going anywhere."

I sob harder. Is this guy for real?

"Calm down, baby. You've got those monitors going ape shit."

I nervously giggle as I try to calm my breathing. Only Decker could make me laugh right now.

In-two-three, out-two-three.

In-two-three, out-two-three.

I practice the breathing techniques Dr. Smythe had once told me would settle me down if I got too upset. I never really needed to use them. I'd turned my feelings off until my dad died, and I saw Decker again.

"I'm so sorry, Decker," I tell him several minutes later, when the beeps on the machine are at a regular pace again.

"And I'm sorry I didn't come after you when you left home. I should have. I'm sorry for a lot of things between us, Case."

I shake my head. "No, I was a teenager basically having a childish hissy fit. You didn't need to uproot everything to come after me when I was just being stupid."

"But I can't help but think–"

"No," I cut him off. "No shoulda coulda wouldas. It's the past, Deck. We can't change it. It all would have happened whether we were still friends or not."

He kisses the back of my head, and I sink further into his embrace. "But I loved you then. I should have gone after you."

My heart melts at his words. "I loved you, too. But Decker, I don't think either of us really knew it back then. In retrospect, it's pretty clear. But at the time, I'm not sure I knew exactly what I was feeling. I don't think you really did either."

"Maybe," he admits after brief consideration. "But you were still my best friend, and I shouldn't have let you go that easy."

"Maybe," I agree just to stop him from beating himself up. "I was gonna come home for winter break. Thanksgiving was too short to go cross country, but I was going to come home at the end of the semester. I wanted to see you. To tell you I was sorry for leaving."

"But you couldn't..." he says.

"I went in the hospital right after Thanksgiving."

"I'm sorry you had to go through that, Case."

I squeeze his arm. "So how is your love/anger ratio doing?"

He holds out his loose hand where I can see it and tilts it from side to side in a so-so gesture.

I laugh lightly. "I *am* really sorry."

"I know you are. I am, too."

"So what happens now?" I ask him. I know he's here laying with me again, but what does it all mean?

"Now, we fight for what we should have three years ago." He kisses the edge of my ear. "But first, you sleep. You need your rest."

I look over my shoulder, ready to interrupt him—not understanding what exactly we're fighting for, or about, since we're here together now. But he presses a kiss to my lips, silencing any words before they have a chance to get out.

"Sleep," he tells me, his tone leaving no room for argument.

I sigh, knowing I owe it to him to just chill out for the night. He hasn't even been here an hour, and we've already been through the emotional ringer. I rest my head on the uncomfortable pillow and settle back into his hold.

"I love you, Deck."

"I love you, Case."

***

Despite the daylight streaming into the window, I feel cold. My body immediately grieving the loss of Decker's warm heat behind me. Where did he go? I can hear voices beyond the curtain, but they're too far away to be in the room. I roll to my back and press the button to move the bed into an upright position.

As I run my fingers through my knotted hair, I wish I had a comb. Hell, I wish I had a shower. Hopefully they won't keep me here much longer. I mean, I feel okay. I'm not in tiptop condition by any means, but I feel well enough to sleep in my own bed and lounge on my own couch.

I wonder if my mom ever came back to the room last night. I fell into a deep sleep after the emotional talk with Decker, so I wouldn't know. Maybe he's out there talking to her?

I reach for the remote on the bedside table and turn on the TV, hoping to find something decent on the tiny wall-mounted hospital television. Flipping through the channels I see that it's all daytime talk shows and soap operas. How late did I sleep? I look at the wall clock, 12:30! Wow. No wonder Decker isn't here, he most likely went to get lunch. He had to be hungry. I am a little bit, too.

A few minutes later, I hear the door open and click shut. "Rise and shine, sleeping beauty," Decker says just before he appears around the curtain, carefully balancing something behind his back. "Hey," he grins when he sees that I'm awake.

"Where were you?" I ask, curious about what he's hiding.

"Aw, did you miss me?" he winks.

"Nah, I got a little more sleep since I didn't have your snoring keeping me up."

He laughs. "Yeah, right. First off, I don't snore. Second, you were out like a light the second your head hit the pillow, and you actually let yourself relax last night. Don't you bring me into your little web of lies."

I giggle. "Whatcha hiding back there?"

He smirks. "Wouldn't you like to know?"

I'm hungry, and I'm starting to smell food, so yes, I would like to know. "Decker," I use my most stern voice.

He shakes his head. "You're no fun." He brings his arm around, and he's holding a brown paper bag. He sets it down on the bed and starts pulling containers out. "I wasn't sure what you'd be in the mood for, and I got the okay from your doctor for all of it, since it's not that shit hospital food some orderly tried to drop off in here this morning. Don't worry, I shooed him away. I'm not letting my girl eat that. I swear they're only trying to keep themselves in business by doling that shit out."

I can't help but smile as I listen to him ramble on and on. He's adorable. I love that he went out and got me approved foods because he didn't think the food they were serving was good enough for me. For *his girl*.

He pulls the wheeled tray table over my bed and sets a few containers on it. "We've got a salad with grilled chicken, no dressing." He looks a little sheepish. "Sorry, but none the dressings they had were on the doc's list. And there is some chicken noodle soup, which he said was probably too high in sodium but he let it go. I can be very persuasive." He winks and sets down some silverware.

"Yes, you can." I'm shocked he spoke with Dr. Smythe about my diet. Shocked and even more in love with him, if that's possible. I pop the top on the salad and start picking at the chicken. "Hey, have you seen my mom?"

"Yeah, she came by last night after you were asleep and again this morning. She stayed at your apartment last night. I called Kate and gave her the heads up."

Kate. The thought of my roommate brings tears to my eyes. I've really put her through hell. I've put everyone through hell. I hope Kate was just being overly emotional last night and didn't really write me off. Decker must see the look on my face because he takes my hand and squeezes.

"Just give her time, Case. She was pretty shook up yesterday."

I nod, knowing he's right. I'm not exactly in the position to be demanding after what I've put my friends and family through. My behavior, my reasons...they all seem so silly now.

"So where is my mom now?"

"She was here for a few hours this morning, then she headed out after talking to Dr. Smythe. She'll be back though. She just went to grab lunch."

I nod, picking apart another piece of chicken.

"You know, it might help if you actually eat it," Decker offers.

I smile shyly. "Right."

I manage to eat the entire salad, even though eating a salad with no dressing is like eating leaves and grass. I know I should be more conscious of the nutritional value of things and their ingredients, but at home when I want a salad, I usually just stick with the light and low-fat options. Case closed. A salad without dressing? Unthinkable!

"You know we still have more to talk about, right?" he says after he clears away the empty containers.

"I know." Decker is standing at the end of the bed, and he gives me a little grin, then grabs onto my ankles and pulls me forward a good foot. "What the hell, Deck?" I'm still sitting upright, so I'm not quite sure what he's trying to accomplish, except taking away my backrest.

His smirk widens as he walks around to the side of the bed, kicks off his shoes and climbs in behind me, pulling my back against his chest. "This is much better, don't you think?"

"The best," I agree, relaxing against my new, Decker backrest.

Chapter Thirty-Eight

Decker

The fact that Casey still willingly falls into my embrace after everything isn't lost on me. I'm at least fifty percent responsible for all the shit she's been through the past few years and somehow, despite the rocky moments, she still loves me. What she told me last night makes me hate myself; I'm not sure how she can forgive me when I don't think I'll ever be able to forgive myself. I was a shitty friend and an even shittier lover. How could I just let her go? How could I let her leave without a trace and do nothing to reach out to her? I'd been so selfish. And she was *pregnant*. With *my* baby. I should have been here.

When Mrs. Evans returned to the room last night, I'd slipped out of Casey's bed, careful not to wake her, and spent a good two hours crying in her mother's arms, begging for forgiveness for getting Casey pregnant and for not being there. I'd felt like a failure of a human being—I still do to an extent. But like Casey had said, and her mom told me there's no sense in dwelling on the shoulda, coulda, wouldas. What matters is what I do now. And now, I'm completely devoted to Casey and making things right. Everything.

I'm going to take care of this girl forever.

"I don't want to upset you, Case. I know this isn't easy to talk about, but just know that nothing you say is going to make me hate you or leave you. I'm not going to lie and say I won't be sad, but know that I'm sad for you, not because of you."

I feel more than see her nod, and I wrap my hands around her chest. She then wraps her arms around mine, firmly holding them in place.

"So...I didn't know I was pregnant." I give her a squeeze to let her know it's okay. "The pregnancy put a strain on my heart, which is why I went into cardiac arrest. If I had known I was pregnant or if I had known about my heart condition, it possibly could have been avoided, but I didn't."

The guilt I feel right in this moment is palpable. This is truly *my* fault. *I* did this to her. *I* got her pregnant. *I* caused her to end up in the hospital. I'd talked with her mom a little more about it this morning, and she'd done her best to knock the negative thoughts out of my head, and while I'm not beating myself up over it as much now, I still feel responsible. And I wasn't here. That makes it so much worse.

"I'm sorry, Case."

"Me too."

I run the tip of my nose up and down her ear. "Can you tell me more about your heart?"

"It's yours?" she offers with a snicker.

I lean forward and gently bite her earlobe. "Funny."

"I have cardiomyopathy."

"Say that in English?"

"An enlarged heart."

"Oh."

"Yeah...oh."

"And they can't fix it?" I ask, knowing it's probably not a possibility as she would have gotten it done years ago.

"No."

"So what happens?"

"It gets worse," she tells me after a moment of silence.

"And there's no cure," I say more than ask.

She answers anyway. "No cure."

I decide it's time to throw out the big guns. "Your mom mentioned a transplant?"

She tenses, ever so slightly, but I still feel it. "A new heart could change things."

So what the hell is the problem? I want to ask, but know I can't. Not like that at least. This is sensitive. So sensitive. But I can't understand why she hasn't jumped on the opportunity to get on the donor list. She's young and otherwise healthy. I don't know much about transplants—nothing, to tell the truth—but that alone seems like it would make her a prime candidate. What is she hiding from?

She answers my unspoken questions. "I'm scared, Decker. I could die during surgery. My body could reject the heart. And all that hope...all for nothing. I don't like the idea of the unknown. Right now, I know what the end result is. I don't know when it's going to be, but I know what it will be."

My eyes sting, but I don't let myself cry. I have to be strong...her rock. But who is going to be my rock? Who is going to be there when she's not? I had a life these past couple years without her, sure, but was I really living? I thought about her every damn day. Half the time contemplating when I would grow a pair and reach out to her. But at least then I still had her, even in that small, indirect way. I knew she was out there, and I'd imagined her happy. But if she was gone? I can't even think about her being gone forever. It makes my stomach turn.

Call me selfish, but I just can't lose her like that. If she won't fight for herself, then I will.

"Case?"

"Yeah?"

"Since we've been apart, you've made quite a few decisions based on what you thought would be good for me, right?"

"I'm sorry about that Decker. I realize now that that was a mistake. I shouldn't have shut you out—shut everyone out. I should have told you and known that you could handle it, that you would have handled it. I didn't think about how devastating it would be for you to suddenly find out that I'd died. Especially considering the way I left home."

"Hey," I say, frustrated she's still talking about her dying. I lean my head over her shoulder and turn her face so she can look me in the eyes. "It's in the past. I'm not going to sugarcoat it and tell you it doesn't suck, because it does suck. I wish I could have been there for you, holding your hand or fighting with you, whatever you needed. There's nothing we can do to change the past, but there are things we can do about the future."

She stiffens again, realizing where this is going, but I don't let her interrupt.

"You made some decisions for me, for my well-being, because you're my best friend and even though we weren't speaking, you still loved me."

"Yeah, and we already established that was a *mistake.*"

I tighten my arms around her, and she wiggles against my hold.

"Yes, you got your turn to be selfish. And now it's my turn."

"Deck–"

"You're going to get a transplant, Casey."

She huffs out a breath, twisting in my hold. "It's not that easy."

"It *is* that easy. When the doctor comes in, we're asking him to put you on the list."

"Decker, I don't want to be on the list."

"Yeah, and I didn't want to be on the other side of the country, in the dark about what the hell was going on with my best friend."

"This is ridiculous," she says, still struggling against my hold on her.

"It is ridiculous. I know you're scared, baby. I'm scared, too. I'm terrified for you and, selfishly, I'm terrified for me, too. But I'm even more terrified of you giving up."

"I'm not giving up," she cries, defeated.

"You are. Casey, I hate to say it because it hurts. It hurts me to even think this," my voice breaks, and I need to take a moment to collect myself. "If you don't get the transplant, this thing is going to kill you. If you do get the transplant, there are risks with the same end result, but there's also a chance. A chance that you'll live. A chance you won't have unless you make the choice to fight."

"But Decker, I feel like all I've been doing is fighting."

"Yeah, but you haven't had me in your corner."

"I can't, Deck," she quietly weeps. "I just can't."

The fact that my girl is so ready to give up breaks my heart. It completely destroys me. I hold onto her tight, nuzzling against the side of her face. She may be giving up, but I won't. I can't.

"Casey, I just got you back. I want to see where this thing between us goes. I want the chance for both of us to make up for our mistakes. I want time, time with you. I love you, and I need you more than my next breath. Please. Please do this for me."

This time I don't hold back—I cry.

Chapter Thirty-Nine

Casey

The sound of Decker breaking apart behind me is my undoing.

"I can't lose you again, Casey. I can't let you go." His words are barely coherent behind his heartbreaking sobs.

How can I do this to him? Is this what I've been doing to my parents? To Kate? Have they been standing strong in front of me and then breaking down behind my back?

Nausea rolls through me at the thought of causing the people I love so much pain. I have been so selfish and ignorant all this time. No one ever said anything...but of course they wouldn't...they've been walking on eggshells around me for more than two years. Probably terrified I'd push them further away or break.

Decker's holding me so tight, but I manage to wiggle free just enough to turn myself around on my knees, not really caring about the wires that are connected to various parts of my body. I straddle his legs and cup his face in my hands.

Desperately kissing away his tears, I tell him "You're not going to lose me. I promise. I'll fight, Decker. I will fight for you. For us."

"I've missed you so much, Case. I don't want you to die. I don't know how I could go on knowing you aren't out there somewhere. Even if you don't want to be with me, please live for you. Please. I just want my best friend back. I want her to be okay."

"I'm right here," I tell him, looking into his glossy green eyes. "Decker, I'm right here. I'm not going anywhere. I want to be with you, too."

He looks at me like he's seeing me for the first time. Like the words I said to him a moment before have finally processed.

"Do you mean it?"

I'm not sure which part he's referring to, but regardless, the answer is yes. I mean every word of it. I nod. "Yes."

He gives me a big, beautiful, Decker smile, white teeth and all, and then leans forward to take my lips in a demanding yet tender kiss. His hands tangle in my hair and the pressure he places on the back of my head fuses our mouths together.

Minutes pass. Minutes filled with kisses, touches, and grinding that is surely beyond inappropriate for a hospital. We've long since ignored the beeping of the machines. If I'm gonna die, what a way to go.

Decker finally pulls away, placing three lingering kisses on my lips before fully separating. His face, still tearstained, has a new look to it. Hope. Love. Adoration.

"Did you really mean it? Are you really gonna go through with it?"

"For you, I will," I tell him honestly.

He places his hand over my heart. "No," he shakes his head. "Do it for you."

I nod as a loose tear escapes my eye. He watches it trail down my cheek and leans in to kiss it just before it hits the corner of my mouth.

"I can't wait to spend forever with you, Case."

I smile and lean my forehead against his. "Me too."

And for the first time in a long time, I hope I get the chance at a forever.

***

My mom finally returns just as I'm finishing up signing the transplant paperwork with Dr. Smythe and the hospital's transplant specialist. Her expression is panicked, probably assuming I'm signing a DNR order. She obviously can't see Decker's goofy grin as he sits on the chair at the side of my bed.

"What's going on? Is something wrong?" she calls out shrilly as she barrels over to my bedside.

Dr. Smythe looks over, having just realized my mother was in the room. "Mrs. Evans," he says with a smile, "it seems your daughter has had a change of heart."

My mom comically looks from the doctor, to the specialist, to me, and back again, her mouth opening and closing like a guppy.

"A change of heart?" she asks, holding her hands up over her own heart.

Decker squeezes my thigh in silent support. "I've just signed the paperwork to be added to the transplant list."

My mom squeals. She actually squeals like a teenage girl who just spotted Justin Timberlake in Starbucks. She rushes over, practically climbing over the transplant specialist, and wraps her arms around me.

She pulls away and caresses the side of my face with her hand. There are unshed tears in her eyes. "Oh, thank God." She looks over to Decker and gives him a big smile. She rushes over to him, nearly taking out Dr. Smythe this time. Decker stands up just before she reaches him, and she practically tackles him in a bear hug. "Oh, I knew you could get through to her. I just knew it."

I'm totally not surprised my mother and Decker had apparently chatted about me and the transplant. Decker basically admitted that much to me earlier. And I should have known my mom would recruit him to bring me back over to the bright side. Not that Decker wasn't a willing participant. If he had known all along, he would have led the crusade.

My mom still has her arms around Decker and now she's rocking him from side to side. As much as I know Decker loves her like a second mom, he's giving me a look that is clearly a plea for help. I should let him suffer for plotting with my mom and roommate, but I love him too much, and I think he's suffered more than enough.

"Hey, Mom, can you get your hands off my boyfriend?" I wink at Decker as his eyes widen.

My mom stills, and then pulls away from Decker. "Boyfriend?" she asks, smiling wide and practically bouncing in place. Not sure if she's speaking to him or me at this point.

Decker looks at me for additional confirmation, as if my words hadn't been enough.

"Boyfriend." I nod my head, smiling at the look of happy surprise on both of their faces.

Decker grins and makes a motion to step towards me, but before he can, my mom's got him in her clutches again.

Dr. Smythe and the specialist quietly tell me they'll return in a few minutes, and slip out the door, leaving us to our freaky little family moment.

"It's about damn time!" my mom screeches once the door shuts. I shake my head in an effort to get my ears to stop ringing and briefly wonder if she's talking about the doctor leaving or Decker and I dating.

"I'll tell you kids what," she says as she finally releases Decker—who immediately hurries to my other side, far away from my mom, and grabs my hand, kissing it gently. "Me, your dad, and the Abrams all placed bets on how long it would take the two of you to get your shit together." She's pointing between the two of us.

I can't quite get past the fact that my mom just said "shit," but Decker is more focused on the gambling bit. "You placed bets? How much?"

My mom throws her head back and laughs. I haven't seen her look this free in a long time, at least not since my diagnosis. Naturally I feel guilty since I'm the primary cause of her stress as of late. But the beaming smile and happy tears that decorate her face cause that guilt to recede. The hell I put my family through is never going to fully go away, but I have to hope it will get better.

"Five hundred bucks!"

"Five hundred dollars? Y'all bet five hundred dollars? On what exactly?" Decker asks, utterly flabbergasted our parents were talking about throwing that kind of money around on us.

"Well, I bet Casey was going to be the one to cave first. Your dad said it would be Decker," she says gesturing to me. "Your mom guessed it would be mutual and your dad said, and I quote, 'those two stubborn kids aren't gonna realize what they've got until they're forty, single, and wondering why they haven't ever found the one.'" She says that last part to Decker.

I am momentarily stunned. Didn't they have anything better to do than to take bets on us kids? Then I quickly do the math.

"That pot is two thousand dollars!"

My mom shrugs as if it's nothing. "We were just gonna give it to you kids anyway. Use it towards your wedding or your first house or something."

A wedding?

A house?

Those are things I never thought I'd have the opportunity to even dream about before.

But now I can. Now I may be able to have all that and more...with Decker.

I look over and meet his eyes. One would think a declaration of weddings and buying houses by a guy's brand new girlfriend's mother would send him running for the hills. But not Decker. He's looking at me with the same admiration that I'm sure is visible in my eyes. He's not running. He's not scared. Neither am I.

For the first time in a long time I'm not nervous and I'm not scared. I have hope.

Chapter Forty

Casey

The past few days were a flurry of activity in my hospital room. Decker spent the night, every night. The nurses eventually caved in to his charm, once they realized he wasn't going anywhere, and brought in a cot so he'd stop sleeping in my bed with me—not that it had helped. He spent every night carefully curled around me in the narrow bed.

Turns out I do indeed have an infection and am now on some heavy intravenous antibiotics. Dr. Smythe checks on me at least twice daily, and the transplant specialist has been in and out going over every last detail of the process, from the wait list to recovery. Each time, Decker listens with rapt attention.

I have to actually force him out of the room every once in a while. He argues that since I have to be here, then so does he, but eventually caves. But that only happens when my mom is present to take his place. She's been staying at my apartment and never mentions Kate.

I miss my roommate. My friend. Since Decker is my boyfriend now, I think I can safely say Kate is my best friend without a turf war breaking out. I understand her frustration with me. In retrospect, I'd be frustrated with me. Hell, I *am* frustrated with me. But I still hold out hope every day that she'll visit.

Hope. That's something I seem to have a lot of lately. And you know what? It feels damn good!

This is one of those rare moments when neither my mom nor Decker is not in my room. My mom hasn't arrived yet and Decker stepped out to get coffee. It happens maybe once a day, but tends to last only a few minutes. I'm flipping through the channels on the TV, trying to find reruns of *Family Feud.* It's usually on around this time of day.

The door opens, still blocked by the useless blue curtain, and I look at the clock. "Wow, seventeen minutes. That might be a record," I say dryly, assuming the visitor is Decker.

My guest says nothing, and I look over to see Kate timidly standing at the edge of the curtain. We look at each other for several seconds, neither sure of what to say. I turn off the TV and set the remote down on the tray table beside the horrid green Jell-O Decker brought from the cafeteria this morning as a joke.

"Casey–"

"Kate–"

We both pause, still taking the other in, and then laugh. It *is* funny. I mean we've been roommates for almost three years and we've never, ever, had to struggle to find the words to say to the other.

"I'm sorry, Kate. I put you in a bad position, not only recently, but ever since I was first hospitalized and that wasn't fair to do. I realize now how much pressure I put on you. How much you must have had to have been on alert with me, not knowing what may happen." My lower lips tremble as I fight back the tears. "How scared you probably were every time you walked into the apartment or knocked on my bedroom door. I'm so sorry." A few determined tears escape and run down my cheeks.

Kate steps over to the bed and takes my hand. "I'm sorry, too, Case." She doesn't tell me "it's okay", rightfully so because it's not. I put the poor girl through hell. "I shouldn't have given you an ultimatum. I kind of just lost it, you know? I was terrified. And I didn't mean to stay away so long; I was embarrassed for the way I acted. Jay, Decker, and your mom finally convinced me that you were probably beating yourself up about it as much as I was and since you couldn't come to me, I should just go to you. So I did."

I smile and squeeze her hand. "I'm glad you did."

She settles down in the chair beside my bed and looks up at me expectantly. "So you and Decker, huh?" she smirks.

"So you and Jay, huh?" I throw back with an equally as saucy grin.

"He's been so wonderful to me these past few days." She can barely contain her excitement, leaning on the edge of the seat. My roommate, the girl I never thought I'd ever see with a guy, has found herself one. And a sexy one at that, if I do say so myself. Not as sexy as my Decker though.

My Decker. Still so surreal.

"That's great. You deserve something wonderful, Kate."

"You do, too, you know?"

"I know," I nod in agreement. "And I've got Decker now."

"I don't think you ever didn't have Decker. That boy is crazy about you." She smiles as she leans back in her seat again.

"I'm kinda crazy about him, too."

"So are you two together now?"

I had assumed my mom or Decker was filling her in on what had been going on. But I guess they left my relationship status out. I'm thankful for the opportunity for some girl talk.

"Yeah. We're together. We're going to see what happens."

She rolls her eyes. "Like we all don't know what's going to happen. Yours is the forever kind of love, Case. Y'all have loved each other your whole lives, in one way or another. That's jump-in-front-of-a-bullet kind of love."

She's right. I'd take a bullet for Decker. And I know he would for me as well. I smile at the thought, morbid as it may be.

"Jeez, you've got that same goofy look on your face as your boyfriend." Kate laughs and I can't help but laugh with her. It feels good to be so damn happy. Even though I'm practically tied to this hospital bed and indefinitely stuck in this room, I feel free.

"So tell me more about Jay," I demand.

Kate gives a shy smile before sharing the details. "Well, I think I told you he's a mechanic..."

I settle in and listen to my best friend animatedly talk about her beau. I smile and laugh along with her as she enthusiastically tells me about him visiting her at the restaurant and standing vigil with her the last few days at the apartment.

It's so great to see her like this. I love that we can share the high of our new relationships with one another. Things finally feel so much lighter. For the first time in a long time, I don't have a feeling of sorrow or yearning for what could have been...because I'm finally living my life again.

Chapter Forty-One

Decker

Everything had been going so well, it's only natural we'd hit a snag. A valve in Casey's heart is not closing properly. The doctor called it regurgitation. Which is exactly what I'd wanted to do when he told us.

His voice is starting to sound like Charlie Brown's teacher. Mrs. Evans is listening to every word with rapt attention. Casey is staring down at her hands, fisted in her lap. And me? I'm pacing the miniscule hospital room like a caged lion. Ready to strike out at the world.

While my heart is ready to beat out of my chest, words like valve repair and replacement are exchanged between Mrs. Evans and Dr. Smythe. Casey is fisting and twisting her hands in her lap, looking about ready to cover her ears and yell "la la la la la" at the top of her lungs to drown it all out. I can't blame her. I'd do it, too.

After three more minutes of the same drivel, I've had enough. I stop pacing and yell for them to stop.

Casey's mom and the doctor pause and look at me, stunned that I spoke out. I usually don't. I'm usually the one at the edge of my seat listening to every word and asking all the questions. But I can't right now. Not when this is so clearly tearing my girl apart. I look over at Casey who still has her head down. The slight movements of her shoulders indicate she's crying. I step over to her bedside and pull her into me, kissing her on the top of her head as she silently weeps into my chest.

"Can we talk outside for a minute?" I ask, looking at her mother and the doctor.

"Sure," Dr. Smythe nods and leads the way out of the room.

"I'll be right back," I whisper, kissing Casey on the head once more.

"What's going on?" Mrs. Evans asks once the door closes behind me.

"You're making Casey upset. If you're going to continue to talk about this, I ask that you do it out here. I mean no disrespect, but it's upsetting her, and I think she's dealing with enough without adding more to it."

"But we need to talk about this. We need to decide what to do," Mrs. Evans pleads.

"I know that." I do. "But all this doctor speak is freaking her out. To be quite honest, it's freaking me out, too."

Her shoulders slouch. "I just want her to have all the facts."

"I'm sure Casey will make an educated decision. But we just got her to agree to the transplant. She's terrified of the surgery, of the risks, now we're going to ask her to have another surgery? I think we need to give her time to digest this."

Dr. Smythe interjects. "We may not have a lot of time. The damage to her valve is extensive. We really need to operate as soon as possible."

"But that's another open heart surgery. We're asking her to have two heart surgeries when she didn't even want to have one."

Dr. Smythe nods gravely. He knows what I know. Given the options before her, Casey may choose not to have either surgery. She's spent the past two years practically waiting for death. Now it may very well be at her doorstep.

What will she choose?

Dr. Smythe has taken Mrs. Evans to his office to continue their discussion. They said they would come back in a little while to talk with Casey about the operation, giving me time to talk to her and see where her head is.

I enter the room and peek around the curtain. Casey is lying back in her bed, looking out the window. The moonlight is reflecting off the raindrops spotting the glass. A dreary sight for a dreary occasion.

I approach her side and take her hand in mine. She squeezes. My mouth opens and closes a few times, not knowing where to start. But before I can put together the words, she speaks.

"I'll do it."

She says it so quietly, I'm not sure I heard her right.

"What?"

"I said I'll do it. I'll do the surgery. I'll let them repair or replace the valve. Whatever they need to do."

I sit down beside her on the bed, always careful of her wires, and gently cup her face, turning it towards me. "Are you sure about this?" I ask, looking into her eyes.

Her eyes, the color of milk chocolate and perfectly clear, look deep into mine. "I told you I was in this whole future thing with you,

Decker. I meant what I said. I'm not going to give up now. Not when I've finally got you. I'm still scared. Terrified even. But I have you and you're all I need."

Fact: Guys sometimes cry when they're happy. Especially when their girl is the most amazing woman on the planet, and she says all the right things to make you feel like your life is complete.

I wipe my eye with a knuckle and lean in to kiss her on the lips, then I rest my forehead against hers. "I love you so much, Casey. You are so brave. So strong."

"I haven't felt very brave or strong. Not until you came back into my life. I guess I was always missing you. You've always been an integral part of my life, and when I didn't have you, it was incomplete. Now that I'm whole again, I feel ready for anything."

My smile stretches clear across my face. This amazing girl is mine. All mine.

"We're going to fight this battle together, baby, and we're going to win."

"We're going to kick my broken heart's ass." She laughs.

"That we are," I agree.

The door opens, and Mrs. Evans calls out "knock, knock" just before she appears around the curtain. "Casey, why are you crying?" she asks when she catches sight of her daughter. Then she looks at me. "Decker, why is she crying?"

I grin her way, and she visibly relaxes. "She's gonna do it."

Casey's mom looks at me quizzically, then looks to Casey, then back at me. "Really?" she asks, holding a hand over her chest.

"Really," I nod, grasping Casey's hand.

She hurries over to hug me, and I sense a repeat of the other day when Casey agreed to the transplant. She's practically choking the life out of me. Better me than Casey, I guess.

"Thank you, Decker. You've brought me my girl back."

I get a little choked up because, you know, like I said, it's okay for guys to cry when they're happy. Mrs. Evans releases me and leans in to lightly hug Casey. No matter how many times Casey tells her mom she's not going to break her, Mrs. Evans is always vigilant. I imagine this is what she was like when Casey was an infant.

"This is great news. I'm so proud of you, Casey."

"I know. Thanks, Mom."

Mrs. Evans holds Casey's other hand, and we share a moment. Each of us holding on tightly to the one girl who links us together...the girl who means the most to us in the world.

Chapter Forty-Two

Casey

Over the past two days, it seems I've been visited by nearly every doctor and specialist in the hospital. I know that's not the case, but it's been a bit intense to say the least. Dr. Smythe prescribed me some kind of anti-anxiety drug that is now pumping through my IV. It has taken most of the edge off, but I'm still scared. Terrified even. I want to do this. For Decker. For my mom. For Kate. But most importantly...I want to do this for me.

The valve surgery is scheduled for bright and early tomorrow morning with Dr. Wyatt. He's been by a few times to check my stats and to talk to us. Us being me, my mom, and Decker. The two of them have barely left my side since I made the decision to have the surgery.

It's both comforting and unnerving that they won't leave because part of me, the petrified part, thinks they're spending all this time with me now in case they can't later— hence the anti-anxiety meds. And the other part of me that doesn't want to be alone is grateful for their vigilance.

It's only me and my mom in the room at the moment. I'd sent Decker down to the cafeteria to smuggle me a chocolate bar. His sad eyes implied he wasn't thrilled with being sent away, but I sent back my own set of puppy dog eyes, and he caved.

"Mom?"

She looks up from the crossword puzzle on her lap and clicks the button at the end of the pen. Yes, she's one of the ones who does the crossword in ink. Not fair, I know.

"What's up? You feeling okay?" she asks when she sees the serious look on my face.

"I need you to do something for me. Something for Decker."

Her eyebrows scrunch up at my request, and she frowns. "Casey, what's this about?" Her voice is a little high-pitched, concerned.

"Please mom, just promise you'll do this for me?" I softly beg.

She looks at me, deep into my eyes. Looking for what? I don't know. Maybe a sign that I'm giving up or about to hand her my last words to Decker.

Apparently content with what she sees, or at least resigned, she nods. "Okay. I'll do whatever you want."

***

"What was that song you were always playing sophomore year?" Decker asks, cuddled up against my back on the small bed.

My mom left about an hour ago to try to get some sleep. I know she didn't want to leave, but I think she could sense Decker and I needed some alone time since he couldn't stay the night in my room tonight. I know I'd see them both in the morning, but saying goodbye to my mom tonight had been hard, and I know it will be even worse with Decker.

"That's not vague at all," I say with laughter in my voice.

"You know the one...it was a pop song, a one hit wonder."

I know the exact song he's talking about, but I'm secretly hoping he'll start to sing it. "I'm not sure."

"Come on, it's the bug song."

"Something by The Beatles?" I suppress a giggle. Next thing I know, Decker's left hand is on the side of my rib cage, and he's tickling me!

"You think I don't know what you were doing there?"

"Stop...it," I plead in between giggles.

"Tell me what I want to know," he demands, raising his voice to be heard over my cackling and the beeping of the machines.

"Fine," I surrender, trying my best to squirm away from him with zero space to work with. "Fireflies."

"That's the one! You used to love that song," he says, settling back into place behind me.

"Yeah."

We're both quiet for a moment, the only sounds in the room are the beeps of the machine and me trying to catch my breath while he rubs circles on my side. There's an elephant in the room. An elephant in blue surgical scrubs.

"Tomorrow is going to suck," Decker says solemnly, finally breaking the silence.

I'm surprised by his words because he's remained so positive since our first night together in the hospital. The feel-good meds are keeping me from tensing up, but not from feeling compassion towards the man I love. My best friend.

I reach up and squeeze his hand. I'm not going to tell him that tomorrow isn't going to suck because I know that for him, tomorrow *is* going to suck. I'll be unconscious and unknowing while he's in a drab waiting room most likely driving himself and my mom mad. That's why I'd asked my mother for that favor earlier today. I had to do something for him. To ease the pain I know will be in his heart tomorrow.

"The procedure will probably be over before you know it." It can take anywhere from three to six hours—the length of a few movies or a really engaging book. That's like no time it all in the grand scheme of things.

"Right," he says, his tone indicating that he's clearly not impressed with my attempt to mollify him. He sighs. "I wish they could knock me out with you. And then wake me up when they wake you up."

I smile at the thought. "Would be nice, I bet. You could probably use the rest."

"I know you're going to be okay...it's the only possible outcome. But Case, I'm still scared."

A few tears escape my eyes. I'm not sure I've heard Decker sound this vulnerable since we were kids talking about stuff that was way bigger than either of us understood. I sniffle and roll over to face him, raising my wired arm over my head.

"I'm scared too, Deck. But everything will be okay," I tell him confidently. "Like you said, it's the only possible outcome. We have forever to get to, right? Forever together?"

"I think it's supposed to be 'together forever,'" he corrects, his eyes nervously darting around my face, as if he's trying to memorize every inch. My heart breaks for him a little bit more.

"No, that was already a given because you're my best friend. But we have forever together to look forward to now. Like this," I say, resting my head against his chest.

"Forever together," he quietly repeats, kissing the top of my head.

Chapter Forty-Four

Decker

The nurses had to damn near pry me out of Casey's bed last night. She had fallen asleep shortly after our talk, and I just held her. I knew I should've gotten up and left, but I couldn't. I knew I should've woken her up to kiss her goodbye, but I couldn't do that either. Telling her goodbye makes me feel like I'm not going to see her again.

I'm sitting off to the side while she and her mom talk to Dr. Wyatt, the cardiothoracic surgeon, and Dr. Moore, the anesthesiologist. I had to step away because I can't hear about it anymore. I usually believe that knowledge is power—the more you know, the less you're afraid—that's absolutely not true in this case.

The more I know, the more I freak out. There are so many risks—no wonder Casey had been reluctant to have additional surgeries.

I'm fighting an inner battle. I feel like a complete asshole for pushing her to have the operation if these are the kinds of feelings she'd been having. And for her, they were probably amplified since it's her life and body on the line. And then the other part of me is telling that part of me to shut up, because the thought of no future with Casey is even more terrifying.

I wish my mom and dad were here. I haven't spoken to them since Casey has been in the hospital because I know that with them being as close to Casey's parents as they are, they had to have known about her heart and not told me. I'd been so angry at them and so consumed with Casey that I'd never picked up the phone.

Now I just wish they were here. I wish my dad would give me one of his manly half-hugs and pat me on the back, his silent but strong way of telling me he's always got my back. And I really wish my mom would hold my hand. I know that makes me sound like a wuss, but I don't care. Sometimes a dude just needs his mom and dad.

The doctors start making their way towards the door, and I tune in just in time to hear them say they'll be back in ten minutes.

Ten minutes.

My heart is pounding in my chest so hard that if I was hooked up to one of those monitors, I'm positive it would blow up.

Casey's eyes meet mine from across the room—those deep, brown pools that so perfectly match the milk chocolate we got from Ghirardelli's days ago. God...that feels like a lifetime ago, but it's only been a little more than a week.

I step over to her bedside and stand across from her mom. Mrs. Evans is holding Casey's left hand and I'm holding her right. My gaze doesn't move from her face, not even when her mom takes my free hand and holds on tight.

No words are spoken for the next ten minutes. We silently hold on to one another and feed off each other's strength and love, praying to anyone who will listen that everything will be okay. That Casey will be okay.

When the doctors return to wheel her down to the OR, I lift her hand to my lips and kiss it—I can't kiss her face, I'd asked, something about germs. "I love you," I mouth.

"I love you. Forever together," she soundlessly says back.

I smile and take a step back while her mom dotes on her one last time, still not taking my eyes off her beautiful face. Memorizing every last detail to hold myself over until she's wheeled into recovery in a few hours, God-willing.

Casey's mom steps out of the way as the staff do what they need to do to make my girl and her bed mobile. I put my arm around Mrs. Evans's shoulders and feel her trembling. She's holding it together about as well as I am, and I know that as soon as that girl is out of our sight, we'll both break.

"We're ready to go," one of the orderlies says.

Casey looks at us, her eyes wide. "I love you both."

"I love you, Case," I say, thankful my voice didn't crack.

"I love you, sweet girl." Her mom's voice breaks on the term of endearment Casey's dad always used for his daughter.

Casey smiles and relaxes back onto the bed. "I'll see you later," she calls out as they roll her out the door.

Mrs. Evans collapses into a chair sobbing, while I fall back against the wall, holding my head in my hands.

Please let her be okay. Please let her make it through this. She has to. She just has to.

***

Thirty minutes later, Mrs. Evans and I are sitting in the waiting room, mindlessly watching TV. They gave us a random number for Casey so we can keep updated on her status. A screen on the wall, which oddly looks like a giant, color-coded spreadsheet, lists the numbers and the statuses. Since we'd arrived in the waiting room, Casey's has said "pre-op" and then "OR." That won't change for a while, but it doesn't stop me from looking to the screen every couple minutes.

A quiet commotion at the door jerks my attention from what is probably my tenth time looking at the status board in as many minutes. I rise to my feet, patting Mrs. Evans's knee as I stand. I move towards the doorway as if being pulled by a magnetic force.

My mom sees me coming and bursts forward, wrapping her arms around me as soon as we make contact. I feel like I'm five years old again, being comforted after skinning my knee or bumping my nose. When I feel my dad's palm firmly land on my shoulder, I tremble and let loose an anguished sob.

"Shh," my mom coos. "It's okay. She'll be okay."

"How did you...how are you here?"

"Maureen flew us out." I pull away from my mom and look over at Mrs. Evans; she hadn't mentioned she'd spoken with my parents.

"Casey asked me to," she quietly tells me, and I nod. It's just like Casey to know I'd need my mom and dad here with me today.

"Why don't we sit?" my dad suggests, and we all follow him to the little alcove Mrs. Evans and I had taken over in the corner. My dad sits beside me and my mom sits beside Casey's mom, holding her hand in silent support.

"How long has she been back?" my mother asks.

I glance at the status board. "Thirty-seven minutes. She's been in the OR for fifteen. Her number is four-one-nine-six-three."

"How long is the procedure?"

"It can take anywhere from three to six hours," Mrs. Evans tells my dad.

He nods and looks to me, his face crestfallen. "Look, son. Your mother and I can't tell you how sorry we are for not telling you about Casey." I look at my dad, I mean really look at him. This man, who has always been my invincible hero, looks like he's aged ten years in the few weeks since I've been home.

"It doesn't matter now, Dad. I know why y'all did it. I might not agree with it, but I get it. Casey and I talked, we worked it out, and it's full disclosure from here on out."

My dad nods and pats my shoulder. My mom and Mrs. Evans both give me watery smiles, each looking apologetic. Yes, I had been pissed at all three of them. Four if you include Casey, and five if you include her dad. But it doesn't seem appropriate to blame the two of them right now.

Regardless, none of that matters right now. What matters is Casey and the fact that she's currently fighting the first of many battles for our future.

***

I jolt from my sleep, apparently woken up by a nearby ruckus. I hadn't realized how tired I was. I look around, trying to get my bearings. As the outside world starts to fade in, I realize I'm alone in the alcove. Where are my parents? Mrs. Evans? I look at my watch, only twenty minutes had passed since my parents arrived. I can't even believe I fell asleep in such a short amount of time.

Maybe they went to get something to eat?

I shake more sleep out of my head and look towards the doorway.

No. No, no, no.

Dr. Wyatt is there.

It's too soon! Casey's only been in the OR for thirty-five minutes. The surgery is supposed to take three to six hours. What the hell is he doing here? He's supposed to be there, with her!

My parents' backs are facing me, but I see Mrs. Evans's profile. Her hand is over her mouth and tears are streaming down her face. She's shaking her head.

No.

Not my Casey.

I slowly rise and take a step towards them, but I feel dizzy. Everything is in slow motion. I shake my head, trying to clear the sleep out. I need to wake up. Maybe this is a dream? A nightmare? Maybe I'll wake up and Casey will be in recovery.

I manage one more step and hear a faint call of my name before blackness takes over.

Chapter Forty-Five

Decker

Four Months Later

"Decker," a feminine voice calls as I step out of the florist.

I turn and see Carrie Miller walking towards me on the sidewalk. Sighing, I curse myself for not having gone to a different florist. Carrie's family owns the little boutique two shops down, and I knew there was a chance I'd run into her here. She could probably smell me coming. The girl has been relentless since high school. Knowing what I know now, I'm glad I never got involved with her.

Clutching the daisies in my hand, I face off against her. Against Casey's high school arch-nemesis. "Carrie," I say coldly.

Her cheerful expression falters, but only for a brief moment before her plastic demeanor falls back into place. "I haven't seen you around in a while."

For good reason, I think to myself. "I've been busy."

"About your friend–" she starts, giving me a sad smile. Fake emotion to go with her fake face. My blood boils at her belittling words and condescending tone, and I have to remind myself that it's not okay to hit a girl.

"I'm not talking about her with you," I scoff. "If you'll excuse me, I'm heading to the cemetery." I hold up the flowers.

"Right," she looks at me with sympathy in her eyes. "Would you like some company?"

Is she kidding me? I bark out a laugh. "Seriously? Did you think I'd never find out the way you and the rest of the crew treated Casey behind my back in high school? Did you think she'd never tell me?"

Carrie's face blanches, and she doesn't say a word. At least she's finally catching on.

"She was my best friend. I thought you all were my friends, too. How wrong I was. How could you do that to her? How could you treat another person so poorly? Someone as sweet and kind as Casey. You're nothing but a bully, Carrie. So the answer is no. No, I do not want your company now or ever. The love of my life is waiting for me, and I don't need a fake friend when I've got that."

Carrie scampers off with tears in her eyes. Serves her right after all the times she'd probably made Casey do that same thing.

"That was pretty cruel," a voice says from behind me, startling me. The voice of an angel. My angel. I turn around and take her in. She's standing a few feet away from me looking perfect in a white sundress, the sunshine making it look as though there is a halo over the crown of her head.

"You're so beautiful," I tell her, taking the few steps to close the distance between the two of us.

She smiles up at me. "So are you," she says, patting my chest with one hand while smoothing my button-down shirt with the other.

Casey's different now. She's still the same girl we all know and love, but having a second chance at life changed her. She's bolder than she was before and today's wardrobe choice is proof of that. The v-shaped cut of her dress exposes part of her scar—something she never would have shown off before. In fact, I never did see the scar from her first open heart surgery until she told me all her secrets in the hospital.

"You ready?" I ask, taking her hand.

"As I'll ever be."

We cross the street, our hands clasped together, swinging between us. This is our new normal. *This* is heaven.

There was a moment four months ago when I thought I'd never experience this—life—with Casey. When I saw Dr. Wyatt in the waiting room that day, I thought it was all over. I thought Casey was gone. The idea had brought me to my knees, quite literally since I'd actually passed out right there on the dingy floor.

What I hadn't realized at the time was that Dr. Wyatt was there to bring us good news—amazing news. Mrs. Evans's tears were those of joy, not sadness. As it turns out, shortly after Casey was put on the table, Dr. Wyatt had gotten notification from the transplant specialist that a compatible heart had become available in another hospital in the city. For whatever reason, Casey was the most convenient candidate for that heart—not that I'm complaining, it's just the whole situation was unreal.

Dr. Wyatt had only made the initial incision by that point, so he'd quickly stabilized her and rushed out to the waiting room to speak with Casey's mom and get approval for the transplant—which of course she gave. It was a miracle. An unbelievable miracle. But it'd happened.

When I'd woken up and they'd told me what was going on, I was overjoyed—hugging anyone who came within a five foot radius. And when Casey had woken up, she'd been stunned silent. She had a new heart. There was no more waiting, no second surgery. It was all done. There was still time for her body to reject the new heart, but all her other woes were mollified. She didn't die on the table, and everything with the surgery went beautifully.

It was rainbows and fucking butterflies.

Recovery was tough. She stayed in the hospital for two weeks and was under close watch for the three months that followed, checking in with her doctors twice a week at first, and then weekly. She hated being so limited, but I kept reminding her that it was essential to our forever together, and she'd settle right down.

Dr. Smythe finally gave her the okay to travel two weeks ago, and we finally got to have our road trip. The route was a little different than the one I had originally planned, this one including the precise proximity to hospitals along the way. Casey had rolled her eyes at that, but I didn't back down. Later on, she told me it made her love me more.

Once we enter into the cemetery, I let go of Casey's hand and wrap my arm around her shoulder, pulling her into my side. It makes us wobble a little as we walk, but I would easily trade my balance for nearness to Casey.

Casey takes the daisies from me as we approach her father's white marble headstone. She crouches down and places the flowers in the small bronze vase in front of the stone. When she stands back up, she leans back into my chest, and I wrap my arms around her, resting my head on her shoulder.

"Hi, Daddy," she starts. "I'm sorry I haven't been by to see you, but as I'm sure you know, I've been a little bit busy. But everything is good, really good. I'm so happy, Daddy. And in case you weren't paying attention last night...I said yes." She looks down, smiling at the sparkling diamond on her left hand, and my heart swells.

"Decker, you better not knock me in the water," Casey warned as I led her, blindfolded, out onto the dock.

The candles were all lit, as planned, and there was a blanket spread out at the end of the dock with some fruit and cheese and sparkling grape juice. Her mom had even laid out her fine china for the occasion.

Once we reached the end, I loosened the blindfold, and Casey gasped.

"Deck...it's like a fairyland," she breathed as she took it all in.

What must have been one hundred candles were set around the dock, glowing in the darkness, some were even floating nearby in the water. My mom and Mrs. Evans had really outdone themselves. It looked much better than I could have ever imagined.

"What is all this?" she asked as she turned to face me, gasping once again when she saw I was down on one knee. "Decker?"

"Casey...I think I knew when I was six years old that I wanted to be by your side for the rest of my life. Back then though, I think I was planning a future of making mud pies and climbing trees." We both laughed. "But nevertheless, you were always right there baking dirt and swinging from branches beside me. Things changed over the years, and it wasn't always good, but in the end it's you and me, side-by-side again. The way I'm certain it was always meant to be. I know this may seem sudden to some, but it's not. We've been working at this for fifteen years and if there's anything you and I have learned, it's that life can be cut short. I don't want to waste another minute, Case."

I nervously reached into my pocket, finding the warm metal with the tips of my fingers. I pulled it out and held it up to her, looking into her eyes. Her hands were covering her face, but her eyes were shining...glowing.

"Casey...I want to start our forever together today. Will you marry me?"

Tears spilled down her cheeks as she nodded. "Yes! Of course I will!" She dropped down to her knees, and I slid the ring on her finger. She gazed admiringly at the two karat *princess cut diamond on a platinum band before launching herself into my arms.*

"I love you," she said, leaving kisses all over my face. Our lips finally connected amidst the cheers of our nosy parents in the background, undoubtedly huddled in the Evans's kitchen watching the scene.

This was perfection. It was everything I could have ever wanted all wrapped up in one moment. With Casey, life would always be perfect.

Casey

"Decker told me he snuck over here yesterday to ask your permission." I sniffle and a few tears escape. "I miss you, Daddy, so much. But thank you. Thank you for bringing me Decker. Or for bringing me to him. You all knew we'd end up together in the end. I'm just so sorry you aren't here...really here...to see it."

Decker tightens his arms around me and tilts his head to kiss my temple. He's my rock.

"We've got to get going, got a wedding to plan and all. We're only home for a week before we have to get back to California. Decker transferred to USF, Daddy. Can you believe it?" I laugh, barely believing it myself.

"Neither can I. Turns out he can't stay away from me." I lean my head against his and rub my cheek against his.

Deciding to finish college in California was not an easy decision for Decker. He was a Gamecock through and through. But the idea of spending another minute away from me while I finish my degree at Stanford was simply unthinkable for him. I'd offered to leave Stanford, but he refused, knowing it was my dream school and he wanted me to live and experience everything I ever wanted since I was so afraid for so long. He said it was a small sacrifice on his part to be with the girl he loves, and this last year in California will be enough time for me to phase out of my post-transplant check-ups. Then I'll be referred to a heart specialist here in Charleston, where we'll get to live happily ever after.

"I love you, Daddy. I'll visit again before we leave." I kiss the tips of my fingers and brush them against the marble.

"I'll take good care of her, sir," Decker says, patting the top of the marker. His gesture makes me love him even more. I didn't think it was possible at this point. Everything he's done for me and with me since we'd reconnected has been completely selfless and amazing. *He* is amazing.

We stroll out of the cemetery, hand-in-hand once again, both of us smiling, both of us happy.

"So where do you want to get married? Here or California?"

I look at him like he's crazy. "Here, of course." Why would I want to get married in California when our history and our families are here in Charleston? Sure we got back together in California, and it will always be special for that reason, but it isn't home.

He smiles as if he knew what my response would be. "Maybe we can put something together for Christmas or spring break?"

I stop walking, the lack of movement causing Decker's arm to jerk back. "What?" he asks, confused.

"I don't want to wait that long," I tell him. "I think we've waited long enough to be together."

He certainly can't argue with that, and he knows it, so he says nothing.

"Let's go to the courthouse tomorrow."

Decker steps so that he's facing me and tilts his head to the side. Now he's looking at me like I'm the crazy one. "Case, you deserve something bigger and better than a courthouse wedding."

"All I deserve—all I want—is you. We can do something bigger when we move back, but I don't want to waste another minute. I want to marry you here in Charleston, and I want to do it now, before we go back to California."

"But what about our moms? You know they'll freak out."

Valid argument, but I have a solution. "No, they won't. They'll be so excited about planning the big wedding that they won't care."

He laughs, nodding his head. "You're probably right."

"Duh, better get used to it," I smirk bumping my hip into his.

"Gladly," he grins, leaning in to kiss me. "Okay, let's do it."

My eyes light up. "Really?"

He nods. "Really."

I shriek and jump at him, his strong arms immediately wrapping around me, holding me tight. Safe. "Thank you!"

"No, thank you!" he says, spinning me around right there on the sidewalk.

"I love you, Decker Abrams."

"I love you, Casey Abrams."

I grin. "I like the sound of that."

We smile against each other's lips, and he sets me back down on the sidewalk. Snatching my hand, he tells me "I told you we were gonna be best friends."

I giggle. "And I'll always share my cookies with you, Deck."

THE END

Acknowledgements

Wow, this has been an experience! First and foremost, I'd like to thank the readers and the bloggers and everyone out there who gave Our Moon a chance and who are now giving Change of Heart a chance. If there weren't people out there who liked and loved Our Moon, Change of Heart never would have happened. So thank you! For me, it was so much different writing my second book. For one thing, people actually knew about this one! They were supportive and encouraging and I didn't feel like quite the island I'd made myself when I wrote Our Moon. To my family - thank you for your support. Those of you who read Our Moon and reached out to me, thank you. It means a lot. Thanks for your encouragement and enthusiasm. To my husband - thanks for reading my stories and for liking them. Thanks for continuously putting up with my crap. To my betas, Meshia, Saleena, and Amanda - thank you for your feedback and encouragement. I appreciate it so much. Amanda, you have been such an amazing friend through all of this and I'm so glad to have met you. To my support team and street team - you ladies rock. Thank you for everything. Your support is off the charts and I appreciate each and every one of you. Thanks for letting me talk crazy to you sometimes, too. Aimee Lukas - I've said it before and I'll say it again, it is so much fun being able to do this with you. I think if anyone else was my editor I'd flip them off at least twice a day, but you make editing fun. Thank you for all your hard work and your friendship. Ginni Hall - thank you for being my sounding board for book-related and non-book-related things. Thank you for your endless support and encouragement. I'm so glad I found you all those months ago. Melissa Allen - Change of Heart wouldn't have teasers if it weren't for you!! Thank you so much for letting me take advantage of your awesome talent. Natasha Carrere - thank you for loving Our Moon and organizing its blog tour, and the one for Change of Heart. Thank you for proofreading Change of Heart, too. I appreciate all you've done so, so much! I'd also like to thank Cassy Roop of Pink Ink Designs for the new cover! As always, you do amazing work! You're a genius. There are so many more people who I've interacted with in big and small ways over the past few months, too many to name without undoubtedly forgetting someone, but I appreciate every single one of you! Everyone who has touched my writing life in some way. Thank you so much.

About the Author

Jennifer lives in South Carolina with her husband and their four fur-kids. She is in grad school, pursuing a Masters in Psychology for Clinical Counseling. When she is not at work or taking classes, she is either reading or writing. Books have always been a passion. She also enjoys spending time with her family, traveling to new places, and music.

Connect With Me

Email: jenniferlallenauthor@gmail.com

Website: www.jenniferlallenauthor.com

Facebook: www.facebook.com/jallenauthor

Twitter: https://twitter.com/AuthorJenniferA

Mailing List:
https://tinyletter.com/JenniferLAllenAuthor

Also by
Jennifer L. Allen

Our Moon (JACT 1)
Hearts in the Sand (Jact 2)

Coming Soon
Right Place, Right Time (Second Chances 2)

Made in the USA
Charleston, SC
05 June 2016